THE HEART OF STONEM MANOR

Lana Moon

BREAKING FREE

Young, rich and careless, John Stonem built a manor on cursed land, and he paid the price with everything he ever loved. He's *still* paying. But now, twenty years later, he thinks he's found the cure.

Single mom Hazel Loveless, too, has been down on her luck, but that's all about to change. She received a surprising invitation to Stonem Manor, home of the city's most eligible—and mysterious—bachelor. Her arrival is the beginning of captivity—and hope. A mystery lurks here, one that must be solved. And while trusting John is not easy, his sensual nature has awakened her own. Both this tortured man and his manor harbor deadly secrets, but through her love Hazel has the power to conquer all and mend two broken hearts.

LOVE FOR THE LOVELESS

"You, not extraordinary?" His words were roughened with passion.

"I'm just Hazel, John. There is no larger-than-life anything about me. I'm a mother. I wanted to be a writer, but all I do is scribble on a notepad. I worked a bunch of lousy diner jobs. And now, I schlep coffee for the St. Jerome paper. At least, I *did*."

"That's far from the truth, which you continue to shield from everyone. Tell me what you write about."

"No."

He brushed his lips against her neck before meeting her gaze. "I want you, Hazel. But I can see the hesitation in your eyes." He leaned closer to her, never breaking her gaze. "Let go of your reservations. Let me make love to you. Let me give you something you've never had."

"I've had sex before, John."

"But you've never made love with a man who would go to so much trouble just to have you."

THE HEART OF STONEM MANOR

Lana Moon

www.BOROUGHSPUBLISHINGGROUP.com

THE HEART OF STONEM MANOR
Copyright © 2015 Megan Bryant

ISBN 978-1942886-41-9

For the real Hazel

CONTENTS

PART I

Chapter 1
Chapter 2
Chapter 3
Chapter 4

PART II

Chapter 5
Chapter 6
Chapter 7
Chapter 8
Chapter 9
Chapter 10
Chapter 11
Chapter 12
Chapter 13
Chapter 14
Chapter 15
Chapter 16
Chapter 17
Chapter 18
Chapter 19
Chapter 20
Chapter 21
Chapter 22
Chapter 23
Chapter 24
Chapter 25
Chapter 26
Chapter 27
Chapter 28
Chapter 29
Chapter 30
Chapter 31

About the Author

THE HEART OF STONEM MANOR

Part I: A Gift and a Curse

"Love is a symbol of eternity. It wipes out all sense of time, destroying all memory of a beginning and all fear of an end."

—Madame de Stael

Chapter One

"You're sure you wouldn't want something closer to the city? Something a bit more settled? There would be a lot of landscaping needed before you could even start building. And that's another concern—"

In the backseat of the town car, John kept his hand on top of his wife's. He was trying—without success—to tune out the incessant droning of their real estate agent.

"—have you considered how difficult it will be to build a house of this magnitude on a small peninsula of land? Maybe this would be better suited for a future project, something further down the road in a few more years. You know, the bridge is the only access point to the peninsula, unless you plan on building a dock and buying a boat."

"Seclusion is exactly what I want, Mrs. Reynolds. If I wanted noise and irritation, I'd have insisted you find a plot of land near my overbearing father." John's tone was biting, and he saw the poor woman flinch.

"Of course. Forgive me, Mr. Stonem. I don't mean to step out of line, but this would be a pretty large project, and you gave every indication you wanted the house built quickly."

"I'm not one to shy away from a large project."

"And you're not taking it on alone." Just hearing his wife's voice soothed his temper.

John was barely twenty; Alison was only twenty-two. He already knew his father's thoughts on the move—thoughts he didn't need to hear repeated by his agent. He also knew his only shot at having a real life was to make a home with Alison far away from the poison of James Stonem.

He'd escaped his father before. As a teenager, he left Stonem Estate to backpack through Europe. His mother hadn't approved. His father, ever condescending, said it was "just a phase John needs to get out of his system."

Then, one ordinary day, that phase ignited into something extraordinary.

Her name was Alison. And at one glimpse, his world of dutiful family obligation was torn apart.

On that sunny day in London, he would see her walking down the sidewalk, not a care in the world. She was devastatingly beautiful—and completely unlike anyone he'd ever know.

She had long auburn hair that burned like fire in the sunlight. Her crisp, white blouse was tucked in neatly to her navy blue skirt. It was a windy day, and as she approached him, a teasing gust blew the sides of that skirt up revealing a very generous amount of thigh.

He caught her face. They locked eyes. And then she smiled at him with those lips—ruby red lips that could sting the heavens.

They didn't speak. They didn't even exchange names. He simply reached his hand out to her, and she took it. There was no reason. But she took his hand and never let go.

It was ridiculous. It was something out of the movies. People just didn't fall in love at first sight. Yet, in a mere moment, he had been struck hard by her. And it wasn't just her appearance that rattled him so much. It was her inability to care about his money or fortune—a notion that his father couldn't fathom. James had never known anyone who couldn't be bought.

His father had opposed the match strongly—as had John's mother. In the end, though, John had won the battle. He married Alison, worked abroad for a year, and now was buying the land necessary to give Alison the home she deserved, and privacy from his family.

John knew he had no business having everything. But somehow he did.

"Ahead is the bridge. You can already make out the peninsula."

The car stuttered over an old iron bridge. Ahead of them was lush greenery, trees nestled against the riverbank, and the sounds of birdcalls and water flowing gently.

"My God. It's beautiful. How did you find this?" Alison's face was pure rapture. He could stare at her forever.

"I'm afraid it doesn't look like much, Mrs. Stonem. It's just a bit more than ten acres."

The town car stopped in front of a row of logs. John pushed open the door and helped Alison out. Along the ground were scattered shards of shiny metal.

"What are all these little pieces of silver?" John watched with alarm as his wife bent down and plucked up several pieces.

"Careful. Don't cut yourself."

"Oh, those are charms," Mrs. Reynolds chimed in. "Gypsy charms from the looks of them."

"Charms?" He looked at one piece that had a jagged edge—like a bent arrow. "They don't look very charming."

"Oh, yes." The woman paused and John knew she was examining his face. He hadn't meant to come off so beastly earlier. He smiled warmly toward her, and to his relief, she seemed to relax again. Then the rambling began. "A little tribe of gypsies used to inhabit a great part of this area for a time. In their superstitions, these charms were hung around land for protection from evil spirits, and they were also said to exhibit healing powers."

"I had no idea you knew so much about gypsies, Mrs. Reynolds."

"I do love history, Mr. Stonem. I'm afraid I'm a sucker for these old stories."

John squeezed Alison's hand and winked, but he noticed she was still enraptured by the silver she was holding.

She finally spoke. "What kind of evil spirits, Mrs. Reynolds?"

"Honey, please don't take this so seriously." He hated superstitions—they were ludicrous. But Alison had always been a believer.

"I want to know, John."

He sighed. He could tell by her tone he wasn't going to be able to change the subject. "Alright, Mrs. Reynolds. Tell us all about the infamous Missouri gypsies, who until about five seconds ago, I never knew existed."

The poor woman flinched again, and he felt a sudden pinch from his bride.

"Johnny!"

"I apologize, Mrs. Reynolds. My wife is spellbound." He leaned over and kissed Alison's forehead. "Please, continue."

Mrs. Reynolds cleared her throat awkwardly before continuing. "They had Eastern European roots, Mr. Stonem, but they kept to the old ways when they came here. As they traveled, they would use silver to ward off evil."

"Fascinating. I've read articles similar to what you're describing, Mrs. Reynolds. Isn't it silver that's said to repel werewolves?"

"You are too right, Mrs. Stonem. The use of silver and other precious metals has origins all over the world. This particular tribe is no exception. And besides these silver charms, they were also known to fashion dolls to hold the lost spirit of a loved one."

"They made dolls? How interesting."

John was getting concerned that Alison was buying too much into Reynolds's fairytale.

"Oh, yes. Many cultures viewed dolls as empty vessels to house lost spirits. Or evil ones."

"So the dolls held souls?"

"That's why so many dolls are made to look so life-like, my dear. Some dolls are used to commemorate a loved one, like a lost child. Others are used to trap energy—or bad spirits—so they can't do any more harm."

"Here I thought we were buying property today. I didn't know haunted dolls and Missouri gypsies were part of the transaction." He felt another hard pinch from his wife.

"I hope my story isn't irritating to you. I always think it's important for a buyer to know the history of the land."

"Well, you've certainly added a layer of mystery to an otherwise boring day of paperwork." He winked at Alison.

"Well, then. If you'll give me just a moment, I'll gather my materials, and we can stop wasting time."

"You are so right, Mrs. Reynolds. Let's not waste any more time." John grabbed Alison's hand and made a mad dash toward the river.

"Mr. Stonem! Mrs. Stonem! Where are you going?"

John pulled Alison carefully down toward the riverbank. It was perfect. No sounds of motors or people. They would be isolated in their own little world.

"Look at the way the land dips the closer we get to the river. I could have a garden back here."

"You can have whatever you want." He was watching her closely. In her eyes, he could see the river's reflection.

"How close could a house be to the river?"

He chuckled at her. "Would you rather have a houseboat?"

"No! But I do have fantasies, you know."

"Oh?" He turned back to see Mrs. Reynolds fumbling inside the car. "And what exactly are you fantasizing right now?"

He had her in his arms; his mouth was tracing the length of her neck. "A *house* fantasy, Johnny!"

"I have a house fantasy. It involves you, me, and very little clothing." He was backing her against a tree. He was backing them both away from Mrs. Reynolds's view.

"What do you think you're doing?"

"Christening our house."

"Are you out of your mind? That woman is just up the hill!"

"She can't see us from here." He was already pushing her skirt up.

"You better be right."

At that very moment, he didn't care. He picked her up and stepped in between her legs. "Well, Mrs. Stonem, welcome home." He clumsily unzipped his trousers, and in the struggle to push them down his thighs, he lost his balance…and pulled both of them into the river.

The heavy splash of water brought Mrs. Reynolds slowly tumbling down to them.

In the water, John caught a hysterically laughing Alison by the waist. "You horny idiot! What are we going to tell Mrs. Reynolds now?"

"Oh, I think she'll get it when she sees my pants hanging off my shins."

"And your sizable member."

"Why, thank you."

After a rather revealing exit from the river, John, with Alison, signed on the dotted line for the very peculiar property. Life was about to explode with every possibility.

+++

In five short months, the construction of the four-story manor was completed. It was in record time, according to the contractor. But John's push for round-the-clock labor and his offer of generous overtime to the workers had been all too necessary. He needed the house finished as quickly as possible. There was a feud brewing between his father and his sister, Laura, who had found herself thrown out of the Stonem Estate. Indefinitely.

Suddenly the home he had built for himself and Alison was also going to include Laura. But instead of being turned off by the idea of living with his troubled younger sibling, John saw it as an opportunity.

He may not have shared Alison's faith in superstitions, but he knew damn well that most men didn't have it all—not the money and the soul mate. It was one or the other.

He saw proof of this in his parents. "Your mother had a purpose," James had said, "and when she served it, she knew she could relax. We had our heir. And then we had your sister. The marriage served us both well." James never spoke about loving John's mother. It was all business. All neatly arranged. Rita Stonem had fulfilled her purpose, meaning she had supplied a son. The daughter was merely a bonus child, but not a necessity.

In fact, though James never spoke the words, John often wondered if his father regretted having Laura. From the time she was born, she was riddled with health problems. Severe respiratory infections. Fluid in her lungs. Asthma that required nightly breathing treatments. Their parents had sent her to South Africa for six years hoping the tropical weather would finally cure her lungs.

It seemed to have worked. Except that Laura had never gotten over being sent away. Especially considering neither parent had bothered to visit Laura while she was recuperating. When she returned to the family, she was thirteen years old. She was a stranger to their parents. Though forbidden to see her lest his studies suffer, John had written to her constantly. After all, she was his sister.

John often had thoughts of saying something to his father—of telling James that it was wrong to send Laura away with no one but strangers to care for her. But his father had been a tyrant, and he thought better than to provoke him. Still, he regretted never saying anything. Even if he had been barely more than a boy.

The damage was done, though. As a young teenager, Laura had been arrested twice for stealing cigarettes from a local shop. She was caught having sex with a caterer at one of James's galas. Now, at eighteen, she had attempted to seduce one of James's oldest associates. Their father had stumbled upon the pair—Laura, on her knees before the man's open trousers—and he immediately cast her out.

"She's a throwback, John," James had said. "If she's capable of this as a child, what the hell will she do as an adult? She's better off locked up or dead."

John was driven and ambitious; Laura seemed perpetually lost.

"Mr. John, I have a room on the second floor set up for Miss Laura, per your request. I'll start dinner shortly."

John nodded at Bennings, his father's butler, who had never married but instead remained James's steadfast employee for the past two decades.

Bennings had been delivered a week before as a "gift" from James. Or, more to the point, Bennings had received another DWI—the worst one yet, as the man had passed out at the wheel and slid into another car. No one was seriously hurt, but the driver of the other vehicle had suffered a broken arm. James paid out of his own pocket to save the old man, but after the ordeal was over—and the scandal squashed—James had thrown Bennings to John. While John had been horrified by the degrading use of the poor man, Bennings seemed much happier to be away from the ill-tempered older Stonems. John had not once seen Bennings take a drink in all the time he had been with John and Alison.

"Thank you, Bennings. Have you seen my wife?"

"I believe she's in the garden, sir."

John wasted no time. He exited the back door and went onto the veranda that overlooked the garden—*her* garden. The river that led to the city of St. Jerome, Missouri, roared on just beyond the last row of tulips. Blue tulips, because Alison said they matched his eyes.

Every living thing in the garden—every flower right down to its color—was to Alison's taste. Red vines that cascaded around trellises. Purples and darker blues that cradled the walkway like some mystical path to the beyond.

How she was able to make everything beautiful and perfect astonished him.

The house had only recently been completed. Mere finishing touches, personal touches, were all that was left. Every inch of the giant manor house contained pieces of John and Alison. Her favorite colors—the deep purples, blues, and reds—were speckled throughout the hallways. John's love for rugged Eastern European art lit up the barren walls in the form of local artist's paintings along with the many pictures of Alison. Their wedding day, their honeymoon, their first day in the manor—their lives together in lovely blown-up Polaroids.

It was an extraordinary house. It was an embarrassingly large house.

"Do you like it?" Her voice was as giddy as on their wedding day. "I think I'll order some shrubs next week."

"I think it's lovely, just as you are."

He grabbed her by the waist and pulled her against him. The sun was brilliantly shining, and he stroked the length of her long hair, hair that was colored like fire. "I don't know what's brighter: the sun shimmering off the river, or this. Kiss me." He closed his lips on hers before she could respond.

"Are you going to write me poetry now, Johnny?"

He gave a firm smack on her bottom. "No way. The pay is shit."

"All business and no pleasure, then?"

"Wrong again." He led her to the bench that overlooked the river. "Come here." He pulled her onto his lap. She gave him a wide-eyed look as he took her hand and put it against his erection.

"What do you think you're doing?"

"I'm showing you what you do to me."

"I already know what I do to you, John Stonem."

He began unbuttoning the top of her dress—her lovely, clingy yellow dress. "John, your sister will be here soon. And Bennings is—"

"Bennings is making dinner. Laura won't be here for at least another hour. And I need you."

He had her dress open and her breasts exposed. "I dream of this."

"You dream of being half-naked all the time? That makes two of us." He dipped his head and suckled her nipple until her hand grabbed his hair and her voice became raspy and deep. "I mean I dream of these moments with you—when we're alone." She was helping him quickly open his trousers. His erection sprang free, and he guided her on top of it. "After all this time, I still can't help it, you know? I daydream about you when you're not here. And when you are—"

"I know. I have an insatiable appetite for you."

"You aren't bored with us yet?"

He answered her by thrusting upwards. She bent her head back, moaning. This was what they needed—this was what they wanted.

And as far as being bored, he didn't even understand that concept. From the first time he'd made love to her, it was as if she marked his very soul, and no other human being on earth would slate his thirst.

It had been over two years, and he was still completely and utterly obsessed.

"John!" She squealed as he peeled off the rest of her dress and flung it on the ground. It was erotic and perfect. His little garden nymph naked and bucking on top of him.

He couldn't stop touching her: her breasts, her bottom, her stomach. It frightened him sometimes how badly he wanted her. It frightened him that she could match his lust with her own for him.

Then the moment took him. He was going into ecstasy. And reality hit.

"I don't have a condom on," he grunted. "I need to—"

"No! Come inside me!"

"Alison!"

Her legs pressed firmly around him as her hands clawed at his back. That was enough. He came, clutching her against him.

"We shouldn't have done that."

"Why?" Her breathy response was pressed against his chest.

"You really want a baby now?"

She looked up at him with her wide, loving eyes. "Having your baby wouldn't be so terrible." She planted a kiss under his chin, and the sensation of her nipples pressing against him was quickly working at arousing him again. "Or maybe it's that you don't want a baby."

He grabbed her hair and pulled her head back, playfully nipping at her ear. "If you want a baby, I'll give you one. I just didn't think the timing was the best."

"Because of Laura moving in?"

"We haven't had much time together alone in this house."

"So this bench-sex symbolizes the last time we'll be together while your sister lives here?"

He bit her lower lip and suckled it hard.

"I'm sure we'll find occasions. Like…tonight."

"Tonight?"

"Yes. I want you in that oversized shower."

She put her finger to his lips. "Tonight you have a final meeting with your father about the gala. It's tomorrow night, you know."

He groaned. "Goddamn it."

"Unless you can put off the great James Stonem."

He knew that would be impossible. Businessmen from around the world showed up for James Stonem's annual gala. All the money went to Stonem Saves—James's foundation for widows and orphans, civil war victims in Eastern Europe.

In a week, John himself would have to go to Bucharest to secure new investors. He dreaded the trip if only because he would have to leave Alison behind. The two had fought about her going, but ultimately, John felt strongly there was too much instability to risk her safety.

"I think James enjoys sending you on these long-distance business trips. I think he's hoping you'll find another girl and get swept off your feet."

He grinned. "Well, you are a cradle-robber."

She playfully pinched his arm. "Yes, my two years of wisdom is *really* influencing you."

He ignored her annoyance. "It's only for a week. Then we can plan a trip."

He saw her smile. "What do you have in mind?"

"Athens? Barcelona? Paris?"

"I'd rather stay here with you. I want to enjoy my garden."

"Alright, my love. Whatever you want."

They were still so young, he thought. Yet, two years of battling his father had given him a new sense of maturity.

Alison, too, had struggled. She had no family to speak of—just a deadbeat father who was slowly drinking himself to death. She hadn't seen him since family services had removed her from his custody at age ten. After being discarded into an overcrowded foster home, Alison ran off. At sixteen, she was cleaning hotel rooms and paying rent on her own apartment. At twenty, when he met her, she was shadowing the concierge for a major international hotel chain and escorting tourists around London for extra cash.

It was an unlikely match. But John never questioned it. Alison called it fate. He hated that word, but nevertheless, he agreed that there was something almost otherworldly about their joining.

"You better put your dress back on." He begrudgingly lifted her off his lap.

"You mean, what's left of it."

It was just as well. As soon as Alison had her backside covered, John heard Bennings calling them inside.

Chapter Two

John sat with Laura in the study. Like John, she had jet-black hair and long legs. But while John preferred to dress in a relaxed fashion, Laura's style was severe. Harsh black eyeliner, bright pink lipstick, and her hair pinned back with messy strands falling around her face. In fact, *messy* was a perfect adjective for Laura.

His heart sank. For a kid just out of high school, she looked so tired and weary—and much older than she truly was.

"You barely ate anything at dinner."

"I'm not hungry."

"Sweetheart, I have to go to a meeting tonight, but I want you to make yourself at home."

"A meeting? You mean with Father?"

He hesitated in answering her.

"Maybe he wants to see me."

John knew that would be a bad idea, but he didn't want to hurt Laura. "It's just a business meeting for the gala."

"Oh, right. The stuffy, hoity-toity Stonem Gala."

"You guessed it."

"So James doesn't ever want to see me again? Just like that?"

He leaned over and stroked her cheek. "You know James. He's a hard man. But Mother has always been more compassionate—at least where you're concerned."

Laura shook her head. "She told me my behavior was nothing short of disgraceful, and that only poor, ugly girls do that."

He smirked. "Well, that isn't true. And while it was maybe a mistake *whom* you did it with, you aren't an ugly or a bad person, Laura. I promise you that."

He heard her choke back a sob. "I just wish I could undo that night. The look on father's face—"

"Hey, it's done and over with. We just all have to move on. No matter what, I will always love you." He gave her a tight hug. "Now go on up to bed. I'll check on you when I get home."

+++

One other thing John knew for sure, no matter what, was that his father could be a superb bastard.

"I can't believe you'd let that little harlot in your house. You ought to give her a plane ticket and get her out of town."

"I wish you'd reconsider. She's so fragile—she's always been so fragile. For some reason, you and Mother ignore that fact."

John watched his father's face turn bright red. He knew he hit a nerve, but he no longer cared about his father's wrath.

"That girl has caused more scandal than I can count. The best thing I did was run her out of this house, and the best thing you can do for her is run her out of yours. She's got to learn from her behavior. Instead, you keep trying to save her!"

They were talking in circles. "Just let it go, Father. Don't worry about Laura. I'll take care of her from here."

"Between her and that kooky wife of yours, I don't know how you continue winning over investors."

He dared to roll his eyes at James. "You should be grateful I'm taking her in. I'd hate for our investors to learn that the great James Stonem kicked out his only daughter for performing an act I'd wager many an unfortunate woman has had to do in order to survive in desperate times. We're supporting not just men, but women and children. Women who were brutalized and used. Now what would people think of Stonem Saves if they knew the founder—"

"Alright, I see your goddamn point!"

"So you'll talk to Laura."

"I will not! But I won't mention the matter again. You can just…handle it."

He shook his head at James. "It's all about the bottom line, isn't it?"

"You just don't get it, son. Life is not about saving everyone—because you can't save everyone. Sooner or later, you have to learn to save yourself. That's your Achilles heel. You love too much."

"I *love* too much? Ha!"

His muscles clenched in anger when he felt his father's hand grip his shoulder.

"Yes, you love too much. You know why I married Rita? Because she was my intellectual equal, because she wasn't clingy, she never asked too many questions, and because, at the end of the day, she wasn't after anything more than stability. If you love someone too much, they can kill you just by disappointment. That's a weakness I can't afford."

"Disappointment? It's human nature."

"I'm well aware of that. Consider what your sister did. Consider what I caught her doing. Mouth wide open… Christ, John. Imagine how I'd feel if I cared about, much less loved, that girl."

John grabbed his coat and headed for the door. "Only *you* would see love as a weakness."

"I'm a realist. Don't be a fool, John. I raised you better than that."

+++

The drive home was heavy with thought and guilt. He wasn't sure what he should tell Laura, if anything, about their father's attitude. She probably already felt it, but to speak it out loud—well, it made the awful truth real.

John was relieved to find Laura sound asleep in bed. He could put off any further discussion until tomorrow. Or, better still, he could wait until after the trip to Bucharest.

When he climbed the steps to the fourth floor, he could hear the soothing sounds of his wife singing. Quietly, he lingered in the doorway. What he saw perplexed him. Hell, it scared him. Alison was gently crooning her song while sitting halfway out the window.

"How many times have I asked you not to dangle yourself out the window?"

"But, darling, it's only one leg."

"Har, har." He kicked off his shoes and watched her slowly pull herself safely back inside the bedroom. He stomped over to the window and slammed it shut. The sound of the river's current sloshing around below added to his aggravation.

"You're in a fine mood."

"Why don't you go out on the balcony? Why do you have to lean halfway out the window?"

"Calm down. I just like the feeling of hovering right above the water when the moon is so bright."

He was horrified. "God, Alison."

"I'll stop if it bothers you."

"You could get hurt. Don't you ever consider that?"

"Why are you so angry with me?"

"Because it's a risk! It's an unnecessary risk! Don't you understand?" He grabbed her by the shoulders and was about to yell some more when he saw that there were tears in her eyes.

What was he doing? "I'm sorry. James is a bastard, Laura's a basket case, and I'm a shitty husband."

"No, you're not." She leaned in and kissed his chest. His arms closed around her.

"If I ever lost you—"

"Where am I going? I'm right here. I'll always be right here."

He scoffed. "Or halfway out the window."

"I'm serious, Johnny. I would never leave you. You need me to look after you, and I need you—"

"Yeah, you need me to yell at you for no reason."

He let her coax him to bed.

"I've never loved anyone the way I love you, John. I didn't even know something like this was possible. My whole life I thought the best I could hope for was some kind of contentment. And then I found you."

John pulled Alison against him. He sighed when she reached back and started massaging his temples. Once again, James's poison had taken a toll.

"Try and relax. We have two more nights before you leave, and I want you to enjoy them." Her voice was soothing his soul—and his temper.

"I keep thinking about what I'm going to say to Laura."

"You don't need to say anything to her. She knows you love her, and she knows what your parents are like. She's a messed up kid, and rehashing the past isn't going to help her."

"You're right."

He sank farther back into the bed, pulling Alison with him. He tried to reach over her to untie the curtain and cover that damn window. His hand missed, barely, and hit something jagged that was hanging off the edge of the headboard.

"Ouch! What is that?" He reached around the headboard and gripped the object that had cut his knuckle.

"It's a charm."

He knew by the cautious smile on her beautiful face that she had felt his body tense up. "A charm? One of the gypsy charms that Mrs. Reynolds was going on and on about?"

"Yes."

"And why, pray tell, is it hanging off our bed?" He could have exploded again, but instead of feeding his temper, he breathed in the scent of her hair and the lavender fragrance that seemed to be permanently implanted in their bedding.

"It's just for protection. I know you don't believe in any of that stuff, but I do. Fate, destiny, love—call it whatever you want, but it brought me to you."

"Now how can I argue with that?" He smiled when she climbed on top of him and nipped at his neck. "Except, does it have to be in our bed?"

"Where else should I put it, my love?"

"Maybe Laura could use some luck."

"I don't know that giving a fragile girl a sharp piece of silver is a good idea, Johnny."

"Point taken. Literally."

John waited for Alison to go to the bathroom and then quickly grabbed the charm.

He quietly tiptoed over to the window and pushed it open. He knew Alison believed in the damn trinkets, but he believed in having control of his own life. And he refused to let his life be dictated by anything else.

He dropped the charm out of the window watched it land in the river.

He slid back in bed and was nearly half-asleep before he felt her sidle up against him.

"Sleep well, my love. Tomorrow night we'll dance."

Chapter Three

The gala began at nine o'clock the next evening, with the Champagne poured promptly at a quarter after. The lights at Stonem Estate were cast bright white. James had gone all out. The ballroom was decked out in gold and deep blue.

John watched as each guest arrived: millionaires who long had business ties with James. Their wives, who all wore that staple, the little black dress. And they all picked lightly at the trays of food circling the room.

The buffet table was laden with smoked salmon plates, spicy cheese risotto, Parmesan-crusted chicken cutlets, and deep-fried green beans with cranberries. He watched his wife eat neatly, mostly of the salmon and risotto, and observe the crowd. Periodically, Alison would catch him watching her and give him a wink.

Laura sat across the table from Alison. Her face was pouting, and her arms were wrapped sternly across her chest. Alison wore a simple white gown—tasteful and elegant. Laura wore a flashy blue dress with shiny beading. John thought the two women in his life were the absolute incarnation of yin and yang.

As the evening progressed, he followed James's lead, mingling and flirting harmlessly with the black-dressed women. Checks for the charity were being written with record speed. James had more than once turned around and patted John on the shoulder. John was the charmer—he made sure his father knew it. In fact, he made sure the entire party knew it.

"There will be generations of wealth and stability if you keep this up, John." James's praise wasn't exactly something John needed. Regardless, he smiled politely at his father. "I mean it. My accountant says we've already raised more than a million dollars, and it's not even midnight yet."

"I guess your accountant gets a raise." He studied James, and for the first time he saw the signs of aging around his father's eyes. His father's harsh, old, gray eyes. And the silvering hair—how had he missed the transformation? For his whole life, John had viewed James as the overbearing overlord. Jet-black hair, which James had passed on to his children, and his steely eyes that were always so domineering and intimidating. Now, suddenly, James looked like an old man. And John understood the role he'd be stepping into. Soon.

"Screw the accountant. I'm talking about the Stonem legacy. Twenty-four wineries in France. Eighteen domestic wineries scattered throughout Missouri and Iowa. Eleven enormously profitable partnerships with some of the best distilleries in the world. All of that has made the name *Stonem* a symbol of wealth and stability. Generations will be taken care of, John, with advisors looking after everything—and us enjoying the spoils. This foundation, this Stonem Saves, it's not just about feeding some starving people in a war. It gives the Stonem name the aura of humanitarianism, and I think that's why you're so driven to pin down every investor for this charity. It does a man good to see his only son doing his part to protect the legacy. This great Stonem legacy—and the heir apparent is standing right in front of me."

"Thank you."

"The future is in your hands, son."

"Father"—he didn't want to ruin the moment, but he had his own agenda—"I wish you'd talk to Laura."

"John, we've been over this. Life is too short to waste it on the wrong people." James shot a sour glance toward Alison. "I have been more than understanding about this ridiculous marriage you've gotten yourself into—and I'll continue to not interfere. But your sister is another matter."

"She's still your child. Just as much as I am."

Now he felt the old man's hand on his shoulder. "No, John. She's not. Whatever failings you think your mother and I had as parents, there comes a point when we all must make our own choices in life. She continues to make the wrong ones, and I won't be responsible for her anymore. And I'd advise you to focus on yourself—and on your family—or she'll hold you back, too."

"Hold me back? Is that how you've always seen her?"

"We all make mistakes in life. I fathered mine."

He watched James walk away, never bothering to look toward Laura. It saddened John, but he knew that James wouldn't change. Ever.

He danced with Alison. Twirled his lovely bride around the dance floor. Mostly, though, he just wanted to take her home and fall asleep in her arms. But as the night wore on, more businessmen showed up. The Champagne was gone. The whiskey was opened.

By the time the gala was over, John could barely stand up straight. He had never been so drunk in life, and he was pitifully grateful for the soft hands he felt steadying him.

+++

The morning sun was beating down on his face with rage. He rolled out of bed and stumbled to close the curtains. Alison's side of the bed was empty. He figured she was angry about how drunk he had gotten—and the only evidence he needed was the curtains pushed wide open.

He'd be leaving in a day for Bucharest. Whatever bad behavior he ended the evening with needed to be put right. With much trepidation, he stumbled into the bathroom and turned the cold water on in the shower.

Downstairs, he saw Alison sitting in the study. She was sipping on coffee and flipping through a magazine. By the look on her face, he could tell she was agitated.

"Good morning," he remarked cautiously.

"It hasn't been much of one," she snapped in response.

"Yeah…I'm sorry about last night. I have no idea how much I drank, but never again."

"I'm not so much worried about what you drank as what you *did*. Do you happen to recall what you did last night?" Her voice was bordering on shrill, and he felt a great sense of shame.

"No, sweetheart. I don't. I'm sorry." He watched her face closely. There were tears in her eyes, but her head shook in anger.

"I'm assuming I was less than gentlemanly."

"Less than gentlemanly," he heard her whisper. And he was suddenly very worried.

"What…happened?"

+++

Alison stood from her chair and motioned for John to sit on the sofa. She was beyond angry.

"I seldom talk about my father."

"You seldom talk about anything from your past."

"Well, let me enlighten you." Her gut reaction was to take a baseball bat to his face, and she knew her tone matched her fury. "I never knew my mother. I don't remember what she looked like, and I couldn't even tell you her name. My father never talked about her except to say we were 'better off.' The rare times he did talk about her, he was drunk—and he still didn't have anything good to say. He was drunk a lot. Many, many times in elementary school I came home and tripped over beer bottles. *That* was my life."

She had hated her childhood. Every moment was just a breath away from her father breaking another piece of furniture or passing out for half a day. "My first day of fourth grade, my teacher noticed a large cut on my arm. She asked what happened and I told her the truth—the whole truth. Dear old dad and I were trying to collect all the beer bottles because it was trash day. He tossed a broken one toward me and missed. My arm was cut."

"So the teacher called child services?"

"I didn't know it was out of ordinary, you know? I thought everyone lived the way we did. And I certainly didn't see anything wrong with a daughter helping her father pick up his mess. But when the authorities came to our house, well, they begged to differ on our definition of normal. I was taken away and placed in a crazy family of religious zealots who seemed to only be looking for a check from the state, not a child to save. I lived there for two years and left. And that was it."

"And what about your father? You never reached out to him?"

She wiped a tear from her eye. "He died a month after the state removed me from the house. And then it was all over. No more family. No more home. It was just me. Me and all those memories of beer bottles." She cupped his chin in her hand. "I will never stop loving you, Johnny. But what happened last night—you can't even remember what you did. And it'll kill me if it happens again."

She felt his arms wrap tightly around her. "It won't ever happen again. I'm so sorry. I'd never do anything to jeopardize us—never!"

She locked eyes with him. "Promise me, John. Promise me you'll never get drunk like that again. Promise me you'll never be reckless like that. Not with us."

"Last night will never happen again. I know you're angry. Don't you want to tell me what I did?"

"No, it's nothing you need to know, nothing that jeopardized your investors."

"But does it jeopardize us?"

She kissed his cheek and felt her own tears—or were they his?—wet her face. "Whatever happened, you didn't mean it. That's all that matters."

"I love you."

She sank into his body, letting his fingers dip into her hips. "That's all that matters, John."

"Will you promise me something?"

She eyed him with suspicion. "What?"

"Don't walk away from me. I couldn't handle it. You are my life, Alison."

"I won't leave you, you idiot. You said it yourself—there's something strange that binds us. Even if I died, I'd find my way back to you."

"Swear it to me." She saw the intensity in his eyes.

"Swear it to you?" She kissed him hard across the lips. "I'll never leave you. If we're ever separated in this life, all you have to do is wait for me. I'll find you."

+++

Alison watched as Bennings pulled the luggage from the closet for John's trip.

"I'll go to the grocery store with you later, Bennings. I want to pick up a few items."

"Yes, Mrs. Stonem."

She frowned, looking at the checklist for John's suitcases. "Can you make sure to pack socks? John never remembers to pack his socks."

"I beg your pardon, Mrs. Stonem?"

She paused and stared at the old man. "Socks, Bennings."

"No, madam. I mean, if you'll pardon me, earlier you and Mr. John were talking. I couldn't help but wonder why you didn't tell him about his indiscretion with—"

"Bennings, after John returns from this trip, I'll have a private talk with him. But I don't appreciate your eavesdropping."

"I'm sorry, Mrs. Stonem. It's just that… I'm terribly worried about—"

"Bennings, I appreciate your concern. I'll handle this."

That Bennings knew, or at least suspect, what had transpired the night before did little to calm her. The truth of what John had done could destroy him. Alison still wasn't sure how much of it she should tell him.

She came to a sudden decision.

"Bennings, if John asks you anything, will you please be silent?"

She saw the hesitation in his face. "If that is what you think is best, madam. You could bear this secret forever?"

"I guess you and I will both bear it."

"And what of the other guilty party?"

"I'll handle it. John does not need to know of this. The guilt and shame would kill him."

Chapter Four

The blasted morning sun soaked John's hotel room in Bucharest. Ignoring the time change, he grabbed the phone on the nightstand and dialed the front desk.

"I need to make a call to the States."

The heavily accented attendant mumbled a reply. John slowly gave the man the phone number he wished to dial. There was a pause before the phone started ringing. But there was no answer.

John ate his breakfast quickly, showered, dressed, and headed downstairs to the lobby.

"Excuse me," he said to another attendant, a young woman this time. "I tried to make a call home earlier. Do you mind if I try again?"

The woman smiled and pushed the telephone sitting on the counter toward him. He dialed and waited. There was still no answer.

After his afternoon meeting, he returned to the hotel. By the international clock on the wall, it would be after eleven in the morning back home. Everyone should be awake.

He dialed feverishly and waited.

Perhaps he was being impatient. Perhaps everyone was outside. The weather could be turning cooler. Alison was probably in the garden. She loved the garden. She loved listening to the river as it rushed along its banks.

There was no answer.

Five hours later, John was trying not to panic. No one was answering the home phone. No one was answering the office phone. His wife and sister should both be at the house. Bennings should be there.

Where was everyone?

At dusk, he was nearly frantic. He dialed the number again as he paced the lobby.

"John?" A barely audible, but still familiar, voice answered.

"Laura? Is everything alright? I've been trying to reach Alison all day." He could hear what sounded like a sob coming from his sister. "What's wrong, honey? Tell me what's happened."

Her sob grew louder. Then the line went dead.

He frantically dialed the house again. No answer.

Within the hour, he was booking a flight home and checking out of the hotel.

Dread filled him. A dread he'd never known existed.

He was running out of the hotel when the concierge stopped him. "Mr. Stonem! You have a call! They say it's quite urgent."

John dropped his bags and headed to the front desk. He grabbed the phone receiver and barely got the word out: "Alison?"

"Sir, it's Bennings."

"Bennings, what in the world in going on? I'm about to get on a plane home."

"Very good, sir. You are…very much needed here."

John was suddenly nauseous. "Has something happened to my sister, Bennings? She answered earlier, but she was clearly very upset."

"No, sir. Your sister is fine." He could tell the man was hesitant with his words. "Mrs. Stonem, sir, she is…not with us anymore."

He struggled to understand the butler's meaning. "Stop playing around, Bennings. Where's my wife?"

"Gone, sir. She's gone…to another world. A better world, sir."

+++

In twenty hours, John Stonem landed in Des Moines. Five hours later, he arrived at the hospital in St. Jerome.

The weather was growing chilly.

Bennings met him at the airport and immediately put a heavy coat on him. John had no feeling, no emotion. He was numb. From the time Bennings called to the time he arrived to speak to the coroner, there was an eerie and growing hollowness inside him.

The hospital corridor was lit up with autumn decorations. It was nearly Thanksgiving. People were visiting loved ones, giving them flowers, words of comfort.

John was in hell.

The coroner met him at the end of the hall. "Mr. Stonem, we don't actually need you here. We just need to know about the arrangements."

"I want to see her."

He saw the coroner flash a worried look at Bennings.

"*I* want to see *her*. And I'm not leaving until I do."

The coroner stood at the entrance to the morgue. "Mr. Stonem, this is not the place to say good-bye."

"I want to know what happened to her. I want to know how a woman her age dies."

She can't be gone. She can't.

"Your wife took a bad fall." He saw pity in the coroner's eyes.

"A bad fall? What the hell does that mean? Let me see my wife!"

"She fell from the window on the fourth floor, sir." Bennings chimed in.

John's blood boiled. "She fell from the window?" His head was throbbing. His eyes could barely focus. "And?"

"And into the river, sir," Bennings finished. "We…couldn't get to her in time. I believe your sister tried to explain—"

"Alison! I want to see Alison!"

"Mr. Stonem, perhaps when you've calmed down—"

"C-c-calmed down?" John was stammering. He didn't care. "I want to see her right now." He tried to push his way around the coroner, but the man blocked the doorway and grabbed John by his shoulders.

"Son, I can't imagine what you're feeling, but you can't see her like this."

"You let me see my wife—and you let me see her *now*!"

He pushed the coroner back and tried to rush around him. An orderly and Bennings grabbed John, pulling him away. "Alison!" he screamed. Fury and pain ignited him. "You said you'd never leave me! You can't leave me!"

Another orderly and a doctor arrived, pinning John to a stretcher. The doctor was dabbing the end of a syringe.

"No! You can't hold me back! You can't keep me away from her! Let me go!"

A third orderly arrived. John couldn't even move a finger. The horrific feeling of being trapped was overwhelming.

Above the chaos, John heard a voice. Soft, murmuring—it was a needed distraction as the needle struck his arm.

"Wait for me."

Then there was nothing. No Alison. No soft, soothing voice.

He was lying in a hospital bed, strapped down like a madman. His wife was gone. His life was in ruins.

The music in his heart halted. The woman who had driven him to succeed and challenged him to be a better man was gone.

His love. The mother of his children. His home. It all lay in shambles.

Bennings had carefully loaded him into the town car by morning. His sister was there. He could feel her squeezing his hand. The sedation cocktail was keeping him from going mad. It was keeping him still and pliant.

Beside him, he could hear Laura cry. He could feel her tears fall onto his arm. "I'm so sorry," she sobbed. "I'm so, so sorry."

He couldn't move, but he could still speak. He could still make a vow. "It isn't over," he whispered.

"Of course not, John. We'll always keep her in our memories." He could sense Laura pulling him closer. But all he felt was darkness.

"It isn't over. She swore she'd never leave me. She swore. It isn't over. She'll come back to me." He squeezed Laura's hand tightly. "She *will* come back. And I'll be waiting."

The house looked oddly the same as when he had left. He thought it would look alien, lifeless. Instead, every artifact of his life with Alison was still intact. It was as if she had just gone to the store, gone for a walk.

The fourth floor was a grim display. Photos of Alison were covered with what looked to be shredded pieces of black curtains.

"I still feel her," he whispered.

From behind him, he heard the footsteps of Bennings and his sister. He turned to face them both. They looked worried; he didn't care. He believed in Alison. He believed in their bond.

"She's not gone. This house is our sanctuary. She's not gone." He started pacing toward the end of the hall. "All I have to do is wait. That's all I have to do."

He pulled a piece of curtain off their wedding photo and started running his fingers over his bride's face. His sister pulled on his arm and he shook her off roughly. He suddenly couldn't hear anything anymore. But when he looked at Laura, she was sitting on the floor crying.

John laughed. He was sure the others thought his laughter was from madness and despair. But it wasn't. This was just an obstacle. He could *feel* her. He could *smell* her. She'd find her way back to him.

All he had to do was wait.

Part II: Dead Hearts and Living Dolls

"Men are simpler than you imagine, my sweet child. But what goes on in the twisted, tortuous minds of women would baffle anyone."

—Daphne du Maurier, *Rebecca*

Chapter Five

Twenty years later
St. Jerome, Missouri

A police siren sounded from the street below her. She could hear it clearly—even though the windows were closed shut. The insulation of the old building was waning, and the windows themselves needed to be replaced. Every time someone opened the entry door to the building, her windows would rattle.

In the other room, her small daughter was giggling, watching some silly cartoon.

The sounds of her laughter crush the emptiest places inside me. The places that blacken out the light. In the thickest fog of despair, one small word from her newly spoken lips and the sun shines again.

Hazel Loveless put down her pen and notepad.

On the phone, her mother was laying into her again. The sirens were all the fuel she needed.

"Oh, great. Has there been another murder in that damn town?"

"Stop it, Mom."

"Does Scotty hear all that commotion?"

"She's watching cartoons."

"Scotty had friends here. She doesn't know anyone in St. Jerome."

"Neither do I, Mom. It's an adventure for both of us. It's a new start."

"Why? Why have you done this? Why have you taken my only grandchild away? Was I such a terrible mother?"

Hazel let out a heavy sigh. It was familiar dialogue. Beth Loveless would never forgive Hazel for leaving South Bend—and for taking Scotty with her. "You were not terrible, Mom. Of course I don't think that."

"I've been reading books, Hazel. Books about people in our situation."

"People in 'our' situation? What does *that* mean?"

"Oh, Hazel, you know what I'm talking about."

Hazel sighed again. It had been the biggest ordeal of her life—and she didn't even remember it. She was barely six when a freak accident landed her in the hospital. For two months, she lay in a coma. The doctors didn't know if Hazel would ever wake up.

"Near-death experiences change a person, Hazel. When you opened your eyes and looked at me, I was so relieved. I thought my little girl would just spring back to her old self. That didn't happen. But we can still work on our relationship. Taking Scotty and leaving the only home you've ever known isn't the way."

There it was. It always came back to that moment when Beth thought she lost Hazel. And then a miracle happened—only the miracle had come with a price. Two months in a coma left Hazel with no memory of her mother, or any other aspect of her life before the accident. Despite all the medications and doctor visits Beth had forced on Hazel, she couldn't remember to this day.

"Mom, I don't want to have this conversation again. I'm fine. Scotty is fine. We'll come visit you as soon as I get some time off."

"And what about her schooling?"

"Mom, Scotty just turned four. Remember?"

"Well, at least tell me you have her enrolled at a preschool. You do have her enrolled, don't you, Hazel?"

"I have to get ready, Mom. I have a big event tonight for the paper."

"Oh, yeah. Some fancy schmancy party with that Stoner guy."

"Stonem, Mom. And he's not some guy. He's the richest man and the most eligible bachelor in this town, in the state maybe, and I somehow lucked out on an invite to his gala."

"Ohhh, a 'gala,' pardon me."

Beth wasn't an easy woman, but Hazel always tried to consider the hell she must have gone through after the accident. When Scotty was born, Hazel's own fears for her child made her more understanding of the nightmare Beth must have endured.

In their home, Beth had rows and rows of pictures of Hazel. Hazel the ballerina. Hazel the tap dancer. Hazel the princess. And then the pictures abruptly stopped. In Beth's display, Hazel grew no older than six.

Those rows of photos were, in a sense, a shrine to a lost child. The child who returned home from the hospital was no dancer. No entertainer. No smiley-faced sunshine child coveted by parents everywhere.

The Hazel who returned home was, as Beth put it, "damaged." She wouldn't dance. She wouldn't sing. She wanted to be left alone in her room for hours and hours. She looked through books. She peered down at strangers passing by on the street below their apartment. And when she was older, she wrote as much as she read. She wrote poetry. She wrote about places she longed to see. She wrote about everything Beth hated—the mother who mourned her living child.

Every event that happened to Hazel after the accident— graduating grade school, entering high school, graduating with honors, giving birth to Scotty—it was all neatly contained in a series of albums that Beth kept in a drawer. They were always kept separate from the glory of that sunshine child who never reappeared, and whose life Hazel could never recall.

She knew Beth could never accept that *this* was just how life was going to be—which was why she had to take Scotty and leave.

"I'm so sorry that your poor waitress mother could never afford to send you off to some snotty private school where they give out *gala* invitations like flu shots. Maybe had you continued dancing, you would have gotten a scholarship somewhere, but I'm not supposed to harp about the past."

Yes, it was definitely better to let Beth get it out of her system.

"And I'll tell you another thing, missy. You might think you've struggled, but I'm the one who worked double shifts at the diner paying off all those medical bills. I would have thought you would try a little harder not to repeat my mistakes. And what do you do? You get knocked up by some piano player."

"Duncan was a guitarist."

"And then you take my granddaughter and move to some wild town."

"It's just Missouri, Mom. Look, I really have to go. I'll call you later, okay?" She tapped the end button on her phone and changed the ringer to silent.

Hazel stood in front of her cracked full-length mirror and straightened her dress. "Okay, Hazel. Don't fuck this up. If you play your cards right, this could be a life-changing night."

Four months she had been in St. Jerome's, and tonight was her big shot. In her hand was an invitation to the annual Stonem Gala, taking place in the very home of Mr. John Stonem, eligible bachelor—and famous recluse. If she could gain access to Mr. Stonem, she could possibly charm him into an interview, or at least a tour of his impressive home. No local or international paper had managed that since before his wife died.

Still, she wasn't fooling herself. Even if she did somehow manage to score an interview, she wasn't a reporter. She was just fetching coffee and doing some light proofreading for the small, local paper. How she got an invite to the event had been nothing short of luck—or someone else's mistake. Nevertheless, she was determined to take advantage of it. She was going to take pictures of the party at the very least.

No one could get a solo interview with John Stonem. But no one was as willing as Hazel to risk anything and everything. If she could even get him to answer a few ditzy questions, that would land her new opportunities. All she had to do was get his attention.

And so she would. She had a four-year-old to take care of. A four-year-old without a father.

Hazel dreamed about getting into reporting. She dreamed of not spending her entire life waiting tables like her mother. She needed to do better. She had to show her daughter that every life had opportunities just waiting to be taken.

When she had seen the help-wanted ad for an assistant to the editor-in-chief of the St. Jerome paper, she had jumped on it.

Her mother had been horrified. "You'll ruin Scotty. You're taking her away from everything she knows!"

"I'm starting a new life for us, Mother!"

"What about her father? What about his rights?"

Hazel had been more than annoyed by the statement. "Do I need to remind you that Duncan has never even seen Scotty, nor has he ever paid one dime of child support?"

"Well, what if he has a change of heart? You can't deny the girl a father!"

Hazel scoffed. "She's better off." And she meant it. Her entire adult life was all about making the wrong choices and choosing the wrong men. And while there hadn't been a great deal of men, Duncan had been the worst mistake by far. A loser who was drunk and stoned half the time, he more or less acted like Hazel's pregnancy was just a minor cold. No big deal.

But two weeks before Scotty was born, reality hit Duncan. He split with no word, no warning, and no forwarding address. Despite this, Hazel's mother still hoped Duncan would "do the right thing."

But Hazel couldn't keep wishing for a man who didn't want to be in the picture, and who certainly wouldn't make her baby his priority.

The job in St. Jerome was a new future, and a slightly better paycheck. And that was the end of discussion—and the end of South Bend.

St. Jerome wasn't exactly paradise, but at least the rent was cheap. *Very* cheap.

"Mommy, I'm cold."

Hazel cupped her daughter's chin and gave her a quick kiss on the cheek before heading down the hall toward the thermostat. It was barely registering sixty degrees. "Shit," she mumbled.

She grabbed the bat that was always leaning against the closet door—the "just in case" bat—and banged on the radiator.

"Mr. Markle," she called, "turn up the heat!" She heard a garbled noise from her landlord, who lived in the unit below. "I've got a kid up here. Please!"

She turned to see Scotty standing directly behind her, her arms tucked tightly against her little frame.

"Come here, baby." She sat the girl on the couch and grabbed a pair of leggings and extra socks from the laundry basket. "Let's get these on you, and you'll warm up in no time."

Guilt plagued her. Maybe if she did score an interview with Stonem, her boss would give her a raise. And in a year, she and Scotty could find a better—warmer—place. *If* she could even get close to Stonem.

"Let's put on your cute red dress. That'll go well with the white leggings."

"Mommy, do I have to go tonight?"

"Four-year-olds can't stay home by themselves. And Mrs. Markle isn't home to watch you."

That was just as well. She didn't like leaving Scotty with the landlord's wife—mainly because all they did was watch TV. But it was cheap babysitting for her very limited salary.

The Stonem Gala, surprisingly, was offering free babysitting for attendees with kids. Hazel liked the idea of being able to check on Scotty on and off throughout the evening.

"Besides," she added, "I think it might be nice for both of us to get dressed up and go out. Don't you?"

The girl shrugged her shoulders. "I guess so."

It was a good enough answer for the moment.

Hazel returned to her bedroom and put on her dress. It was a Kmart special, but it was all she could afford. At least the green complimented her reddish-brown hair and the black heels gave her a couple of extra inches. But the back of the dress was clingy, and it showed the outline of her underwear a little too clearly. She mimicked her daughter and shrugged, and then kicked off her panties.

She hoped John Stonem would see a woman who could stop him dead in his tracks.

She had a very odd feeling that tonight would be the start of something she'd been waiting for her entire life.

Chapter Six

Caterers were rushing in and out of the grand entrance to Stonem Manor. Bouquets in shades of blue were hoisted over the archway. The same flowers were being positioned as centerpieces atop the gold tablecloths.

The host of the evening's events was leaning stiffly against a banister, watching as the workers frantically assembled the various tables while the caterers were clattering about in the kitchen.

Next to the host stood the old butler. The host regarded his weathered and weary-eyed companion with concern. He gently nudged the old man.

"Isn't this a bit lavish for what will be a very short evening, Bennings?"

"It is exactly as you requested, sir."

"I want all the guests gone before eleven. Can you see to it?"

"Yes, sir. Everything will go as planned."

"The cab vouchers were sent, right? *All* of the vouchers, Bennings? We don't need any accidents."

"Sir, all of the vouchers were sent out."

The host nudged his employee again. Old Bennings, loyal and faithful, wouldn't let him down.

"I want the staff gone by eleven as well."

"The arrangements have all been made. I suppose one old man can clean this enormous house by himself."

The host caught the sarcasm. "Cheer up, Bennings. I thought you were dying for some peace and quiet around here after all this upheaval."

"Of course, sir."

"I'm getting tired of this myself. I think this will be our last gala."

"Oh, but, sir—you've been so energetic this past week."

The host patted the old man firmly on the shoulder. "I guess it's that familiar chill in the air, Bennings. It puts an extra pep in my beleaguered step."

"Your sister phoned earlier, sir. I told her you were unavailable."

"Yes, she's been hounding me for days. I feel an unwanted visit is impending."

He saw the sudden panic in the old man's eyes. "There's no way to put her off, then?"

"I'll handle her. She won't disturb anything."

"I hope not, sir. She sounded very suspicious on the phone."

"She was born suspicious. If she calls again, I'll talk to her. Her presence isn't exactly needed here. I'm dying for some quiet time. And with my sister, it will be anything but quiet."

A worker strolled by both men carrying boxes of toys.

"I'm still not quite over her last visit, sir. Her behavior was most unbecoming. I was quite relieved when you threw her out."

"You sound like my dead father. And anyway, Bennings, can you just make sure everyone leaves relatively early? I'm sure to be plagued again by all those weepy-eyed women with dyed red hair. It gets old…after about an hour. And, of course, no interviews."

"Very well, sir. I'll take care of everything. I have a hopeful feeling about this year."

He wasn't quite sure what the old man meant. He only knew that in a few hours, the dazzling decorations would be gone, the servants would be on holiday, and he would have quiet once again. Living in torment, he thought, was easier when one was alone.

+++

The cab ride to Stonem Manor took nearly forty-five minutes. Hazel was grateful for the cab voucher—courtesy of the gala— especially when the meter hit a hundred dollars and kept going. The clouds above were gathering, and in the distance she could hear thunder.

Beside her, Scotty was holding her raggedy doll and humming an obnoxious little song. But she was happy and hadn't complained the entire ride.

"Are we almost there?" Hazel asked the driver.

"Nearly, ma'am. I have to watch the road to the bridge, though. It gets slick in the rain." He rolled his window down halfway and sniffed the air. "But I think we may luck out on the rain for now."

"I hope so."

From her purse, Hazel pulled out her notepad and pen. Several pages were filled in with various poems and nonsense she had scribbled.

Her mind dazzles over painted faces and dandelions.
On cold nights, her eyes draw to the stars.
Their light, the warmest touch.

She paused to daydream about another life, another reality. A moment in which the lost memories of her youth and the vibrant disappointment of her mother didn't cloud the desperate joy she clung to.

From behind came a familiar caress. A protective arm around my waist with the
faintest cologne tickling my nose. A grip so firm yet loving that goose bumps covered my skin from head to toe...

A man—she was daydreaming about a man! She smirked at herself and tucked her notepad back in her purse. The cab ride became bumpy, and she was surprised to see that Scotty still seemed unmoved by the entire journey.

Everything—hers and Scotty's futures—would be determined by this night. She felt that truth in her bones. She should have been scared to death, but she wasn't. She had a curious feeling that luck would be on her side.

As the cab drove across the bridge that led to the house, a strange sensation came over her.

"Save him."

The voice was so firm and abrupt it nearly made her leap from her seat!

"Sorry, did you say something?"

"No, ma'am," the driver answered.

She eyed Scotty, who was still playing with her doll.

The car pulled toward the front of the mansion. The front entrance was lit up. Limos, Jaguars, BMWs, and a fleet of other cars Hazel could never afford in a million lifetimes were parked along the lengthy driveway.

She suddenly felt extremely out of place.

The driver opened the door for her, and she stepped out, Scotty following right behind her.

"Give me your hand," she said to the child.

Without hesitation, the little girl obeyed. In Hazel's other hand was the invitation.

Maybe they would recognize immediately that she didn't belong. Maybe she would be turned away at the door.

Still, she couldn't shake the feeling that she was expected.

"It's now or never," she whispered to herself as she climbed the stairs to the front door. "This is for a better life, a better way."

She rang the doorbell. A chill went up her spine.

Fate ushered her in. A flood of blues and golds filled her vision. The grand entrance was dazzling. And beyond the entrance was a man standing on the candlelit staircase. His face was shielded in shadows, but Hazel felt certain he stared right at her.

Chapter Seven

Hazel awoke in a room she didn't recognize. Harsh whispering echoed from the hallway outside, sounding like a stampede inside her ears. The pressure building in her head—she could have vomited from the pain.

"Shut up," she murmured. At once, the whispering stopped. Her head throbbed and her body was sore and shaky. Slowly, she lifted herself up from the pillow and surveyed her surroundings. She fully expected to see someone—anyone—in the room with her.

But she was alone.

A giant canopy encircled the bed. Directly across from her was a cherry oak dresser that stretched along the wall. Candles were placed on top of the dresser, and their light danced around the vast space, highlighting the impressive size of the room. Large rugs with intricate patterns were hanging along every wall. Her tiny, two-bedroom apartment could fill the entire bedroom three or four times.

Sheer black curtains with gold drawstrings shimmered in front of one massive window beside her bed. She crept toward it, pulling back the fabric in hopes of recognizing whatever was outside.

Water splashed against the riverbank below, and she was certain she was three or four stories aboveground—three or four at least.

The abrupt opening of the door made her jolt. She turned to see an elderly man standing in the doorway.

"Oh, thank goodness, madam. I'm so glad to see you're awake. Mr. Stonem did want you to see a doctor, but with the bridge down, I'm afraid there's no safe way into the town at the moment."

"What bridge? Where am I?"

"This is the Stonem Manor, madam. You were in a taxi crossing the bridge to the mainland when the bridge began to collapse."

A sudden stroke of terror hit her. "My daughter! My daughter was with me! Where is she?"

The old man put a hand up as she stumbled toward him. "The young girl is quite alright as well. Mr. Stonem is entertaining her in the study."

She heaved a sigh of relief.

The events of the evening were foggy, at best. She remembered packing a bag for her child, she remembered Scotty singing inside the cab on the way to the mansion, and she remembered ringing the doorbell.

She reached for her purse, which had been placed on the dresser. Inside, a damp and crinkled invitation was sticking out of her notepad.

Stonem Gala
You are cordially invited to attend John Stonem's yearly tribute
To his beloved late wife, Alison Stonem.

Of course. The Stonem charity event. Her head pounded as more memories flooded back at the speed of light.

She remembered dropping Scotty off at the side door, where a woman was signing in children who would be staying for the event. She remembered seeing a large flat-screen TV, small colorful tables with books and puzzles, a snack area, and row upon row of toys. Scotty had been overjoyed to escape inside the dizzying room—far away from the more subdued adult event.

Then what happened?

She had taken about a dozen pictures, but she hadn't gotten near Stonem. He was surrounded by a crowd of women, most of them dyed redheads, for some strange reason.

A storm was building. The lights began flickering. Guests were quickly ushered out of the house. Hazel heard the nervous chatter of the guests. If they didn't leave fast, they might all be stranded at Stonem Manor. A cab was called for her and Scotty.

Then her mind grew foggy again.

"The cab driver? He was not the same man who drove me here. I can sort of remember an older gentleman? Is he alright?"

The man only shook his head. "We don't know what happened to the driver. He was not in the taxi when we got there, madam. As it is, we were only just able to pull you and the child out of the vehicle before the bridge fell. You had hit your head quite hard against the window. It was quite dark. The child's cry was what guided us to you both in time."

"So the driver's dead?"

The man shrugged. "We were having some difficulty with the landline earlier, but once the phones are working properly, Mr. Stonem will report the incident to the police. Meanwhile, your daughter is downstairs, madam."

Hazel grabbed her purse and hurried toward him. "Take me to her, please. I need to see my little girl."

In the hallway outside the bedroom, candles lit the way. As if reading her mind, the gentleman offered, "The storm knocked out the electricity about an hour ago. The generator is on, but only in the master study and kitchen. That is where your child is."

She was grateful for his kindness—and grateful they had both been saved—but her heart was still hammering against her chest. Scotty was not much more than a baby. How terrified her little girl must have been! "I'm sorry. I don't even know your name."

"Bennings, madam."

"Well, Mr. Bennings, you have no idea how appreciative I am. If anything happened to Scotty—"

"She is quite safe, I assure you."

Those six words—or maybe it was his soft, soothing voice— began to calm her. The hallway, though, seemed to stretch on forever. Truly, she had never been inside any home so immensely overwhelming. The ceiling seemed to stretch to the sky, but in the candlelight, she could make out finely detailed paintings of a man and woman, seeming to circle around each other. Against the walls, instead of the beautiful rugs that had been hanging in the bedroom, there were mantles with pictures and more paintings.

Near the end of the hallway, she saw a row of what looked to be mirrors placed along an elaborately carved mantle. The mirrors were covered partially with a piece of black cloth. She paused, lifting up a thin piece, seeing a half-shattered image. "Why are the mirrors covered up?" she asked at nearly a whisper.

"It is better not to ask some questions, madam. The stairs are just beyond. Then you'll be with your daughter."

There was a chill to his words, but her concern remained fixed on finding Scotty.

Blissfully, they were descending the stairs. And from a distance, she could hear a child's laughter. *Her* child's laughter.

Bennings opened the door to a study. Soft lighting glowed on the walls, and she could see immediately that the high ceiling here had the same artful decoration as the one upstairs. She saw the back of a man who was bent over, and then spotted the light brown pigtails of her child poking above a chair. The man was holding two dolls. One was smacking into another. The child was roaring with laughter.

"Scotty!"

The little girl bolted from her chair.

"Mommy!"

Mother and child embraced tightly while the two men stood back. Hazel examined her child's face, arms, and legs for any signs of injury. But despite the horror that the girl must have witnessed, she didn't have a mark on her. Her smile and giggle brought much relief.

"Miss Scotty was amazingly lucky. She escaped with no injury. It was you, my dear, whom we were very worried about."

At the sound of his voice, Hazel turned to face the man who had been entertaining her child for God knows how long. He had thick, dark hair that was graying on the sides and a heavy silvering beard. His eyes sparkled a deep blue, and he smiled warmly.

"I'm okay. A bit sore, but I feel much better now that I have Scotty."

He reached out his hand to her. "I'm John Stonem. I think you've met my butler, Bennings."

She nodded. "I'm Hazel Loveless." She shook his hand.

She suddenly remembered the dashing John Stonem from the gala last night. The immaculate custom-made suit he wore was worth far more than a year of her meager salary. Fawning women in designer dresses shadowed him all evening. She couldn't get within ten feet of him. And if she was honest, she didn't want to—her confidence had failed her. He had everything. She was a nobody in a world of somebodies.

But now in the study, he was far less intimidating. He looked just as attractive, just more subdued in his casual attire. She thought she caught him looking at her strangely for a moment, but he released her hand and carried on.

"Mrs. Loveless," he began.

She cut him off. "Please, Mr. Stonem, just call me Hazel."

He smiled warmly again. "Then I must insist you call me John."

She smiled back, but her head was still full of confusion. "John, when did the accident happen? How long was I upstairs?" She watched the men exchange a look, and immediately Bennings left the room.

"It's nearly six in the morning. The bridge collapsed just before midnight."

She had an oddly apprehensive feeling that made her march to the other side of the room and pull back the curtain. "It looks so dark for being morning."

"The house sits on a peninsula. This time of year, when the weather is damp, we often get fog. Sunlight and most daylight are unfortunately at a minimum."

She stepped away from the window.

"Are your phones working? I'd like to call my mother and let her know what's happened."

He frowned. "I'm afraid the phones have been down for most of the night. But if you'll write down her name and number, I will have Bennings keep trying." He pushed paper and a pen into her hand. She scribbled down her mother's information, though the uneasiness she felt only increased.

"Would you like to add your husband to the list? I'm sure he's very worried about you both."

Ha. She had to stifle a laugh. She hadn't married Duncan, much less seen him in years.

"I don't have a husband."

John nodded, and then took the note and left the room.

Hazel turned her attention back to her daughter. "What have you been doing? Have you slept at all?" The little girl shrugged. "Are you hungry?"

"Nope. I ate pancakes. Benny made pancakes."

"Well, don't worry. We're going home soon."

Scotty hugged the doll she was holding—an eerily lifelike doll. "This is better than home. I have all these toys here."

"Scotty, that doesn't belong to us."

"John says I can have her! Please don't make me give her back."

Considering the trauma the child likely experienced, Hazel wasn't going to put up much of a fight. "Alright." Her thoughts returned to John. He was kind, but still there was a sense of unease in the house, a peculiar feeling Hazel couldn't quite shake. "We really need to get going, baby."

"No, Mommy! I want to stay!" Hazel saw the girl's eyes twinkle as she clutched the doll.

"But, baby, this isn't our home. Don't you want to go home? Don't you want to see your nana?"

She heard the door open suddenly.

"I'm sorry, Hazel. Bennings is still trying, but the phones are not working."

"Is the bridge the only way out of here? Is there no other route?"

"I'm sorry. The bridge *is* our exit. If the weather were clear, I could take you into town on my boat. It's eighteen miles south by water to St. Jerome. Too risky today, though."

Her mind was getting jumbled. She felt herself beginning to panic. "Will the bridge be repaired soon? When do you think the weather will clear?"

"Hazel"—he took her hands into his—"you are quite safe here. I'd really rather you rest before I took you out on the boat. The water is unpredictable right now. And you did hit your head pretty hard." He led her to a bronze-colored sofa. "Why don't you relax? I swear that you and your daughter are safe here. Bennings will let us know when the phones are back online."

Phone. Of course.

Her hand plunged inside her purse. Her cell phone. Why hadn't she thought of that sooner? In her desperation, she emptied the entire contents onto the floor. But her phone wasn't there.

"What's wrong?" he asked.

"My cell isn't here. Maybe it fell out of my purse upstairs."

"You were clutching your purse when I pulled you out of the car. It's possible it fell out in the crash."

She felt defeated. "You might be right." She paused, staring at him. "You pulled me out of the car?"

"I grabbed you. Bennings grabbed Scotty. You were unconscious."

Was she just being overly paranoid? Still, it was the twenty-first century, for goodness sakes! How could the phones be down and the electricity be off *and* her cell phone be gone?

"What about you and Mr. Bennings? Could I use either of your cell phones?"

He gave her a warm smile, but she saw that disappointment was looming. "I'm very sorry. I've never had a use for them unless I'm traveling, and Bennings is a true Luddite."

Hazel was stunned. "Neither of you have a cell phone?" She slumped down in the middle of the sofa.

"I have one in my office in St. Jerome, but I rely on the landline when I'm home. Cell phone signals here can be sketchy, at any rate. I'm so sorry."

She should have known. The entire house was like a tomb.

"Hazel, would you like something to eat? Or some tea? You're very pale."

She did feel kind of weak, come to think of it. And disheveled. Beside her on the sofa, Scotty had fallen asleep. "I guess I shouldn't wake her."

"I have a guest room upstairs next to yours that is all made up. Why don't I put her to bed?"

He raised a hand to graze her cheek. The concerned gesture frightened her. She looked into his eyes. Those deep, blue eyes. There was nothing in his demeanor that was threatening. So why did she feel so uneasy?

Before she could answer him, John scooped up Scotty and carried her to the staircase Hazel had descended earlier. Tired, she followed. The long hallway seemed even longer this time. Hazel paused between the door to her room and the guest room. The wall that separated the two was very long—as if another door and another room were between the two.

"Hazel?"

She turned her attention back to John, pressing a hand to her uneasy stomach. When John finally opened the door to the guest room, she had to lean on the wall for balance.

Inside the room, there were two twin beds: toys on one, fresh bedding on the other. The room was nowhere near as elegant as Hazel's, but it was airier and lighter.

He placed Scotty gently on a bed, then shut the door quietly and led Hazel back into that gorgeous bedroom.

"There's a bathroom to the right."

She stumbled toward a side door inside her room. In the bathroom, there was a claw-foot bathtub. Black and white tiles checkered the floor and walls. Drippy candles were lined along the sink and near the window. She stepped inside and saw an uncovered mirror. The green dress she'd worn the night before clung to her body. It was wrinkled and dirty. Her hair, which had been neatly pinned up, now hung around her shoulders in messy waves.

She felt the way she looked: disorderly and dirty.

"Can I run you a bath?" His voice was soft and soothing. If he was faking concern, he was doing a damn good job of it.

"No, thank you." she mumbled. "I can manage."

"Your dress…seems somewhat worse for the wear. If you want to leave it on the rack, I'll have Bennings collect and clean it." He opened a small chest next to the toilet and pulled out towels. "When you're finished, you'll find fresh clothes on the bed. Take your time."

Even though she had declined his offer, he nonetheless started a bath for her and dumped in some bath salts. The aroma of juniper and lavender filled the room. "If you need anything, just give a shout. It won't take long to gather new clothes for you."

He shut the door. She waited for the outside bedroom door to close before disrobing and slipping into the tub. She gingerly sank down into the water, feeling the bruises on her legs and back. The smell of the bath salts did make her feel better, though. It was so pleasant and soothing. She reached for one of the bottles to read the label. Maybe she could pick up her own bottle at Walgreens?

But the label was in French. She sighed. John Stonem was a very wealthy man. No doubt he entertained more than a few ladies in this giant house. And no doubt he spared no expense in making their stay as luxurious as possible.

He had been tending to Scotty so sweetly. Maybe her worry was misplaced. Maybe he was just a bachelor who preferred a more secluded existence.

She tried to remember what she had learned from the slight amount of research she had done before the gala. She was cursing herself for half-assing the job. But Scotty had been fighting a fever the week before, and she had been struggling to get caught up on work.

John had lost his wife twenty years ago in some freak accident. They were both very young. He never remarried, but lived off the old family money. The Stonem name had been well known in the area for over half a century. They owned several wineries in the Midwest, as well as overseas.

What else could she remember?

The gala that John hosted had been dedicated to his wife since her death two decades earlier, and all the proceeds from the event went to a children's charity. But John never had children.

Was that it? Was that all the research she had done?

Disappointed, she slumped deeper into the tub. The water was steamy and felt so good. She began to relax. Every muscle seemed to have clenched up in the accident, but the salts and the heat were working wonders. She could have stayed in the tub for hours. But when she heard the bedroom door open again, her body tightened up immediately.

It must be John delivering those clothes.

She waited for the sound of the bedroom door clicking shut, then grabbed a towel and stepped out of the tub. Her head was still throbbing, and her legs were a little wobbly. She cracked open the bathroom door to make sure no one was lingering in the bedroom. To her relief, she was alone.

On the bed, there was an array of clothes: a purple satin nightgown, a long blue dress, a shorter brown evening gown, and a cottony cranberry dress.

In a separate pile were robes, cardigans, and slippers. She grabbed a white cardigan and the cranberry dress. The dress was a little tight around the bust, so she tied the cardigan around herself.

Peering out the bedroom window, she was surprised at how dark it still looked outside. She lay down in that oversized bed again, thinking she'd just close her eyes for a moment. But the heaviness of the night's events, along with the headache from hell, exhausted her. She drifted off to sleep once more.

Chapter Eight

John Stonem paced the long hallway where his two guests rested. Several times each hour, he couldn't resist checking on Hazel, watching her take deep breaths in her sleep. Seeing her occasional twitch. He felt compelled to keep touching her forehead, checking for a fever or any other signs of distress.

Bennings entered the bedroom to scoop up the dress Hazel had worn the night before. John was careful not to look in his direction. John was too angry. And yet, as angry as he was, he couldn't take his eyes off the sleeping woman before him.

"Sir," the old man whispered, "shall I send this out to be cleaned?"

"Bennings, I could care less what you do with that dress," John said, never looking away from Hazel's sleeping form.

"Sir, perhaps if you'd let me explain—"

"Explain what, Bennings? Explain this?" He held his arms out toward Hazel. The terseness in his tone made the old man walk quickly from the room.

John followed him and quietly shut the door to the bedroom. In all the years he had known Bennings, he had found the servant loyal and trustworthy. He had no words for what the man had done now.

"Dear God, man. Are you drinking again?"

"I'm quite sober, sir. If you'll just hear me out—"

"I'd have to be insane to listen to you now, Bennings. What in the hell did you do?" He wanted to scream at the old man, but used all the restraint in him to keep his voice steady, lest he wake both woman and child.

"I just wanted to make right what was undone." John was sure Bennings saw the horror in his face, for he continued quickly, "You can't deny her face, sir. You can't deny her mannerisms."

John pulled a woman's wallet from the pocket of his jacket and removed the driver's license from it. "You can't deny *this*, Bennings." He flipped the license toward the man. "This woman was born twenty-six years ago. Alison has been gone for twenty."

"I…may have missed that part, sir." His butler's agonized voice made John want to throttle him. "But you must admit her resemblance is uncanny. When I saw her the other day at the grocery store, I'll admit I may have gone overboard."

"Overboard? You think?"

Just last week, Bennings had excitedly texted John pictures of a woman he had seen in St. Jerome. John had scrutinized them closely but hadn't held out hope. So often a pretty society woman would show up at the Stonem Gala. A redhead, usually. Wearing clothing and makeup similar to Alison's. Unfortunately it wasn't too hard for these women to find Alison's photos online, even though the newspaper articles they accompanied had been published some twenty years ago.

It sickened John. It sickened him the few times he physically gave in—all for the sake of feeling something, *anything*.

But he never felt anything but relief once they were gone.

It was Alison's fault. It was her fault for loving him so much, for making him love her so much, and for marking herself so unapologetically onto his soul. He still couldn't move on.

And here was some poor, innocent woman Bennings had lured to the manor.

Hazel Loveless. Her face was so mesmerizing he was hesitant to leave her side. Her voice—oh God, her voice! But it was impossible to believe, wasn't it? After two decades of silently roaming the halls of his house like a madman, half grief-stricken and half furious at being left so suddenly.

In all the years of grief he endured, the only person on earth who had stood by him was Bennings. It was Bennings who had changed the sweaty sheets of his bed when he'd scream out her name in the middle of the night. So many nightmares of seeing Alison fall—watching as though he were somehow there—but always too late to save her.

Bennings had been there for him. And now, the product of that loyalty lay just on the other side of the bedroom door.

"Bennings, I want to know exactly how you got her here. I want to know what caused the accident."

"I took care of everything, sir."

John groaned. "I know you took care of everything. You always take care of everything, but right now, Bennings, for the sake of both our lives, I need to know exactly what you did."

"I may have compromised the brakes in the taxi."

John's jaw dropped.

"The bridge was wet, sir. I was driving quite slowly, but I'm afraid I lost control of the vehicle. It slid into the loose barrier—"

"The one that needed replacing?"

"Yes, sir. And in hitting the barrier, the bridge began to give way."

"Bennings!"

"Sir, you did not speak with her once at the gala. I couldn't let her leave just yet."

John's stomach was in knots. John had heard the crash. Hazel's was the last taxi leaving. When he got to the taxi, his heart sank at seeing the woman in the backseat. Pale, petite, with strands of red hair swept across her forehead. Had Bennings not rushed him to pull her out of the backseat and get off the bridge, John would have been tempted to climb there and just hold her.

But that was madness.

"Then what did you do, Bennings? Besides stealing her wallet and cell phone, I mean."

"I flipped the circuits off in the electrical box."

Again John's jaw dropped. "You mean the electric is fine?"

"And I disabled the landline phones, sir." John heard definite remorse in that last statement.

"Bennings, I don't even know how many laws you've broken!"

"Sir, I couldn't be sure when I saw her at the grocery store, and you were keeping her at such a distance during the event."

"Because it was too much. *She's* too much!"

"But if she is your wife, sir?"

"Inviting her for tea didn't sound like a more reasonable approach?"

"Forgive me, sir. Something compelled me to do this."

"Something compelled you to kidnap a woman and her child?"

"Yes!" The old man's vehemence made John take a step back. Never in his entire life had Bennings raised his voice. "When I saw Miss Hazel, I felt strongly that I must find a way to get her here. Beyond that, sir…I don't know."

John was completely horrified. Never in his life had Bennings done anything remotely this outlandish. At least, not since Bennings had stopped drinking. Yet it was now clear the old man had gone completely off his rocker. A premeditated kidnapping? What was he thinking?

+++

As soon as Bennings confessed to his actions, he felt a grotesque level of guilt. Yet, for two decades he watched John fall into an ever-growing hole of despair. Bennings could stand it no more.

"I'm going downstairs to repair the phone lines, Bennings. I don't think you comprehend the situation you've created."

The butler watched his employer descend the stairs. John had been a bright boy who quickly grew into the role of a powerful young man. But the death of his wife had crippled him. The occasional one-night stands only added to John's depression. When he spotted Hazel in the store, Bennings felt it was fate—and fate was something that Alison had believed in.

Now that John knew the truth, he had to assume John would use Hazel's cell phone to call the police. If only John could see what an opportunity he had been presented with. Bennings had seen the look on John's face when he saw Hazel. And what he had seen was a sharp glimmer of hope. With the phone line cut, and neither man having a cell phone inside the house, Bennings had also given John the gift of time.

If John would see it that way, and Bennings wasn't too sure of that yet.

Bennings worried that John had lost his mind dwelling in the house for so long. This was his last hope. New life for John, and new life for the house.

Bennings suddenly saw a tiny shadow down the hallway. "Miss Scotty?" he whispered. "What are you doing awake?"

The little girl crept toward Bennings. He saw the caution in her eyes. "I'm not tired anymore. Where's my mommy?"

He picked up the girl in his free arm while balancing a long candle in the other hand.

"Your mother is resting. Do little girls still like ice cream?"

Scotty made a giggling noise as they descended the stairs once more.

"Benny, how long is me and mommy staying here?"

At the bottom of the stairs, he blew out the candle and walked toward the kitchen. He took one more careful look back, and then opened the breaker box and flipped on the circuits. Light spilled into the kitchen before them.

"I think, Miss Scotty, that you will have plenty of time to explore your new home."

+++

John crept back upstairs and checked on Hazel again. She was sleeping deeply. He hoped she slept for a few more hours. He had a lot to figure out before he could look into those golden eyes without falling all over himself.

Quietly, he pushed back one of the rugs against the wall and opened the door hidden behind it. His bedroom—also elaborately decorated—glowed. He had forgotten to turn off the lamp on the end table.

Beside his bed sat a large manila envelope. He poured out the contents. Hard copies of the pictures Bennings had taken were scattered across his desk. So was a copy of Hazel's birth certificate. He hadn't completely brushed off Bennings's tale. In fact, he had obsessed over those pictures for weeks and nearly hired a private investigator—until he saw her birth date. Hazel had been born six years before Alison's death. There was no way she and Alison could be the same woman.

"What a hateful way to remind me of all that I've lost," he murmured as he shuffled through the pictures. "All the genetic combinations in the world, and you had to bear her goddamn face."

It was happenstance. Or fate.

And now she was in John's house. In the adjoining room. Sleeping soundly. And safely.

The little girl, Scotty, had been a surprise. He hadn't much experience with children, yet she had taken to him and Bennings quickly. He wondered what kind of life she and Hazel were leading.

He wondered if Hazel already suspected something was off.

John was going to have to think fast. Bennings had done something unbelievably stupid, but the idea of losing the old man to a prison sentence was too much to bear. Bennings already had a record for drunk driving. One old man acting out of the goodness of his heart with *no* record was one thing, but one old man who crashed a car and kidnapped a woman and child when he *did* have a record was quite another.

St. Jerome was a small town with a long memory. The woman whose arm had been broken in Bennings's crash was the daughter of the mayor. And presently, that particular woman had been campaigning to throw the book at repeat drunk driving offenders. Bennings had been sober for twenty years, but that wouldn't matter to a bitter woman and a small town overrun with drugs.

After all his years of solitude, how many good friends did John have left in the legal profession? One? None? Soon Hazel would discover the electricity was working fine and that the phones were back online. He needed to find a way to contain the situation.

Vibrations from the end table brought him around. Hazel's cell phone. He hit decline, and then pulled the SIM card and battery out of the phone.

Bennings was his only true friend in the world. He had made one hell of a mistake, but John was going to try his best to save him—even if that meant taking the fall. In that moment, he made his decision: Hazel could not leave the house.

John opened his laptop and began drafting an email. It was to Hazel's work from Hazel's own email address. No matter that he had to hack into her work computer. Wasn't kidnapping a far worse offense? The first step was to alert her employer of her sudden need to take a leave of absence—indefinitely. The second step was to handle her mother. That would be tricky.

The third step, he would have to somehow keep Hazel and Scotty in the house until he had a solution that would guarantee Bennings's safety. Judging from the third-rate clothes that Hazel and Scotty wore, John had a good idea what that solution was.

Downstairs he found Scotty asleep on the sofa in the study, and Bennings in the kitchen polishing silver. Polishing silver—as if he hadn't just committed a string of felonies.

"Alright, Bennings," he began, "I'm going to fix this for you."

"Sir, I know you are very angry with me. I'll confess to Miss Hazel. I'll tell her everything. She should know that it is I who is the monster, not you."

"No, Bennings. It's too risky. If my plan goes wrong, you could go to jail."

"*Your* plan, sir?"

"I'm commandeering this kidnapping, old man. Just trust me, and I'll fill you in on how we're going to fix this. And Bennings—don't deflect from the story I'm going to tell you."

Chapter Nine

At dusk, Hazel finally woke up. Her head felt better, but she was still weak. And hungry.

On the long dresser sat a tray. She got up and investigated. Bananas, pears, blueberry muffins, water, and juice were laid out. She couldn't recall hearing anyone come inside the bedroom, but nevertheless, she downed the water, a muffin, and a banana.

From outside her window, she heard an animal howl. She was immediately reminded that she was stuck in an isolated location. With her daughter.

Grabbing a candle from the dresser, she left the bedroom in search of Scotty. The hallway was pitch black, but she did remember Scotty's room. To her dismay, though, the room was empty. One little twin bed was unmade, and there were toys all over the floor.

"Scotty? Where are you?" she called up and down the hall. The room next to Scotty's was locked, but the room after that was not. She held the candle in front of her and looked around. A wardrobe was against one wall, and a large dressing mirror hung along the other side of the room.

"Scotty?" She reached for the wall to guide her, as the windows seemed to have heavy tapestries plastered against them. "Are you in here?" Her hand glided along a switch. On instinct, she flipped it upwards. Light spilled out of a chandelier above her. She closed her eyes, blinded by the brightness. When her eyes adjusted, she opened them wider.

The room clearly belonged to a woman. There were racks of clothes—dresses, gowns, and pantsuits in an array of blues, purples, and reds. Every rack was color-coordinated. She stood frozen for a few minutes, taking it all in. Then she saw the initials engraved at the top of the wardrobe: *A.S.*

And she knew.

Alison Stonem.

She looked down at the dress and cardigan she wore, and she realized the ugly truth. She was wearing a dead woman's clothes.

"My God," she whispered.

The pieces were coming together in her head. The clothes she was wearing. The lights that were clearly working.

"Beautiful, isn't it?" The voice directly behind her was startling. She turned and faced John Stonem. "I don't come in this room very often. You've given me a reason to open it back up."

"John," she gasped, and immediately felt sick. "Th-the lights seem to be working now." She tried to step around him, but he was a man of some size. Tall, with wide shoulders, large biceps. He clearly kept in shape.

"Yes. They are working fine," he answered. He gave her that same warm smile—that deceitful, warm smile. "Feel free to pick out whatever other pieces you like."

"No, that's alright, John. The pieces you put in the bedroom are fine. Anyway, if you don't mind, I'd like to make a phone call." She was trying desperately to keep her voice from trembling. "I think Scotty and I have taken up enough of your time and resources. You have a lovely home. A very, very lovely home. But it's time for us to go now." She was babbling. She knew she was babbling. But thankfully he stepped aside so she could get out of that room.

"Scotty?" She stormed back to the child's room, even though she knew her daughter wouldn't be there. "Scotty? Come on, it's time to go!" She stared back at John, who simply stared right back at her. "John, c-could you help me find Scotty?"

He didn't answer.

"John?" Her heart was pounding. It felt as if someone had sucker-punched her. "John, what's happening?"

"Hazel, let me apologize now for what's happened, and for any confusion you're feeling. But the reality of the situation is far more complicated than you can imagine."

Chills soared up her spine. He walked to a portrait that had been covered by a black veil.

"John, please tell me where my daughter is."

He ignored her, and yanked the veil off the portrait. Her heart sank.

It showed a woman in her wedding dress. Red-stained lips, soft eyes, auburn hair. It was almost a mirror image of Hazel herself. Almost.

She was cursing herself for not even bothering to Google a picture of Alison Stonem before the event. Suddenly all those dyed redheads made sense. Of all the research to half-ass...

Hazel took a step back from John. "She's very lovely."

"*You* are very lovely." His words were no longer soothing but ominous.

Dread filled her. The man was clearly insane.

"That isn't me." She stated the fact bluntly. Perhaps too bluntly.

He stared at her intensely for what seemed like an eternity. It was as if he was weighing his options, or trying to make some atrocious decision.

He paced toward the portrait. "This is Alison. My wife." All at once, he seemed to forget Hazel was even there. "We married young. I was eighteen; she was twenty. My parents were against the match, but I fell hard as soon as I saw those golden eyes."

Hazel decided to feed into his memory in hopes of sneaking an escape behind him in the hallway. "What happened to her, John?"

"We honeymooned all over the continent." He reached his fingers to the bottom of the portrait and stroked it firmly. "When we returned, I had this house built for her. Every nook and cranny was built to her delight. Every whim was catered to. She had that bewitching effect on me. I could never say no. Never." He stared briefly at Hazel, who stopped cold in her tracks.

"And that over-indulgence cost her her life."

Chapter Ten

"What do you mean, it cost her her life?"

His tone was frightening. Good god! Had the man killed his wife?

"Alison enjoyed sitting at the window and listening to the water break against the riverbank below. She'd pop the window wide open and lean halfway out of it. It scared me to death." His voice broke. She watched his expression change from worry to heartache to anger. "We took vows, you see. She was always a bit of a gypsy. A bit superstitious." He turned to face Hazel again. "She promised that we would never part. Ever. And so when she fell…" He swallowed hard and looked away.

"She fell from the window?" Hazel's heart sank.

"I wasn't even here. Bennings found her. And my sister."

Despite her fear and anger, compassion seeped through. She reached out to touch his arm and give him a friendly pat. "I'm very sorry, John. It must have been awful."

He was still lost in a trance, she could tell. And she felt an urgent need to find Scotty that far outweighed her desire to comfort this man who had lied to her and was possibly hiding her child. The candlestick she held earlier was sitting in the doorway behind her. She silently stepped back and grabbed it.

It was only an ounce of courage she needed. She had to be brave—for Scotty. She needed to take a deep breath and strike. "I'm so sorry," she murmured.

Then, to her horror, he turned around abruptly and faced her. In one swift move, he grabbed the candlestick and ripped it from her grip. The force of his movement momentarily knocked her off balance.

But it was John Stonem's face that paralyzed her. If looks could kill, she was dead meat. "Don't try anything stupid. You're a guest in my house right now. That can change to prisoner if you do anything like that again."

+++

John was quickly descending the stairs. He paused just once to motion Hazel to follow him. He couldn't believe what this had come to. He was threatening her now?

He could hear Scotty in the kitchen with Bennings, but he stopped at the base of the steps to face Hazel. He saw the fear in her eyes. He hated that look. Couldn't stand to see it in those goddamn golden eyes that held him transfixed. "Look, I know what you must think of me, but until I come up with a game plan, you're going to have to trust me."

"Trust you?" He could hear the fury in her voice. "You kidnapped me and my child!"

He flinched at her words, but he had a duty to Bennings. And her face… He had never felt so many emotions rolling over him at once. "I promise you that I would never hurt you or your child."

"What exactly do you want? I don't know you. After what's happened, I don't want to know you. I just want to take my kid and get the hell out of here!"

And there was the rub. Until she was calm, he couldn't let anybody go anywhere. "I'm not locking you up. You are free to roam the house and the garden."

"Just not free to leave? You do know this is illegal, don't you? Or are rich men truly above the law?"

"The bridge is down. The only way out of here is by boat. Do you see the clouds outside? A winter storm is coming. The last thing you want is to be stranded in the river on a boat with a young child." He drew a breath before making the most disturbing statement of his life. "In any case, you aren't leaving until I'm done with you."

His tone was raw and biting. It wasn't in his nature to frighten anyone, especially her, err, someone with that face—but it was Bennings's future, and his own, at stake.

"What exactly is it that you plan to do, Mr. Stonem?"

"It's simple." He took a step toward her; she took a step backwards. "You're going to stay with me for one month, and in return I'm going to make you a very happy woman."

+++

John Stonem was a madman. As Hazel held her small daughter in the bedroom she now viewed as a cage, it was clear to her how dismal her predicament was. Because she bore the face of John's wife, John had gone to great lengths to kidnap her and Scotty.

And what would happen to them now? What did John mean about making her a happy woman? A sickening feeling had hit the pit of her stomach when he uttered those words. Then as fast as he had said them, he spirited her and Scotty back upstairs. No, there were no locks on the door, but it seemed clear to her that she was to stay put.

Her only reassurance was Scotty's obliviousness. Scotty liked the old man Bennings. Hell, she liked John, too. She saw no danger in either man. But Hazel saw plenty to fear in John.

The soft snores of her child brought her to her feet. She carried Scotty to the bedroom next door and gently tucked her into bed. She returned to her elegant prison and paced with her thoughts. John Stonem was a powerful man. John Stonem was an attractive man. He could have anyone in the world. He was probably used to having women fall at his feet.

The very notion twisted Hazel's stomach, but if she could negotiate freedom…if giving herself to him would buy a way out for Scotty, she'd do it. She'd be disgusted with herself, but she'd do it.

In the chair by the window sat her purse. She pulled the notepad out of it and grabbed a pen.

At day's end, I dream of that dancing child. The child who made the stars cry.

The child whose mother still weeps. Now I weep.

Hazel discarded her borrowed attire, put on a robe, and climbed into bed. A thousand times over, she considered bundling Scotty up and making a run for it. But where could she go? The bridge was out. She had no idea how adept she'd be at using a boat. John's warnings on that score scared her to death. And anyway, her body hadn't nearly recovered from the accident.

It seemed to take forever for her achy body to get comfortable enough to fall asleep. The events of the evening and her worry over Scotty kept her head from resting. Her heart was heavy with fear and doubt. What if John never let her go?

As if the house itself could feel her fears, a heavy dose of lavender and juniper filled her senses. Her breathing calmed, her limbs went lax, and the most delectable pillow cushioned her weary head.

She could hear water flowing gently along the riverbank. And birds—they sang loudly and brightly. Her skin was warm, as if sun-kissed. She saw blurs of blues and reds and purples.

Then, all at once, the birds stopped singing, a chill fell over her, and the water surged on, though angrily now. The colors faded away. There was only blackness.

Her mind was filled with a voice—a peculiar voice. It was almost familiar, but the whispering was so faint she could not make out a single word.

She tossed and turned under the covers. The voice grew louder, more demanding, and suddenly she could hear it—she could hear *him*.

"Come to me." A male voice—young and wild. *"Let me in. Let me save you."*

Fear enveloped her. The voice was menacing, and every syllable made her head throb that much harder. Then the voice changed. It was softer. Lower. And much more charming.

Her mind was diving into a cloud of confusion. It was like a veil had been placed over her eyes. The voice…it begged her again. *"Let me in."*

"Let me go," she murmured in response.

She tried to open her eyes. She tried to make herself wake up.

"Let me in. I'll take you away from all of this. I'll bring you home."

"Home," she murmured.

"Come home." The voice grew in insistence.

She could not answer. Her breathing became deep and rhythmic.

But even in this odd state, she was aware that this wasn't right. It wasn't natural. Why couldn't she open her eyes? Why couldn't she snap out of this dreamy state?

"Let me in."

Just the sensation of energy washing over her was driving her mad.

But it was wrong. She felt it in her bones. She was stuck inside a waking dream.

"No." She fought for the urge to kick her legs up, but she couldn't move them.

"Come home." The voice moved around her from ear to ear. Then it changed again. It was no longer charming, but full-on danger.

And with three words, it brought her back to reality. *"Where is Alison?"*

She shot up in bed, still panting. And, suddenly, she knew she was no longer alone. A frigid chill swept over her. A black cloud that hovered above the canopy started falling below. Falling toward the floor. Falling toward her.

At the foot of the bed, the cloud gathered. Slowly, the figure of a woman appeared. She wasn't very tall. Her face was covered with long hair. Hazel could just barely make out lips—they moved rapidly as if the woman was trying to speak. A dark gown clung to her form, and as Hazel remained transfixed on those erratically moving lips, a single long finger jutted out from the woman's hand, reaching toward Hazel.

"Go away," Hazel whispered. Panic was freezing her in place. "Keep away from me!"

The woman—and her finger—remained unmoved by Hazel's pleas. And those lips, lips that quivered and shook, terrified her. Hazel looked to the foot at the bed as the woman placed her other hand on top of the mattress, indenting the bed with her weight. A cold chill ignited through Hazel's spine.

"No!" she screamed at the top of her lungs. "Scotty!"

The figure disintegrated before her eyes. Hazel gave a final guttural scream before slamming her face back into her pillow.

She heard heavy footsteps rushing toward her. And suddenly there was a hand on her arm.

"No!"

Chapter Eleven

"Hazel! Wake up!"

John pulled Hazel off the pillow and forced her to face him. Her eyes were wild, and her entire body shook with fear. She pointed at the foot of the bed.

"A woman!" John looked in the direction her wobbly finger was pointing. "There was a woman right there!"

"There's no one in this room but you and me. We're alone."

"No! She was here! She was climbing onto the bed! She tried to touch me!"

"Hazel, what the hell are you talking about? There's no one here." John was trying to keep a calm tone, but she was bordering on hysteria.

"I couldn't move. I couldn't get away! And she just…faded away!"

"No," he whispered, pulling her into his arms. "There's no one here. It's only you and me in this room. No one else."

She sobbed wildly. "Her lips were trembling!"

"What?"

"Like a movie that's being fast-forwarded! They were moving too fast, but there was no sound!"

He wiped the tears away from her cheeks. Guilt filled him.

"This is my fault." The statement was more to himself than her. "Hazel, I'm sorry about earlier. I lost my temper."

She pulled out of his arms and stared at him blankly. "Why are you so calm? I'm telling you there's a crazy woman in your house— a stranger—and you're apologizing! My daughter is in this house!"

"Hazel!" He shook her. "You had a nightmare. I'm sure it's because of the present situation, and for that, I am sorry. But my hand to God, there is no one here."

"I saw her, John. I saw her as clear as I'm seeing you now. It was not a nightmare!" She pulled away from him again, holding her robe together as she scooted off the bed.

"Hazel, let me help." He stood up and met her at the other side of the bed. He held his arms out to her. "Please, come to me."

She shrieked and scooted back onto the bed.

"What the hell is wrong?" He was utterly confused and growing impatient.

"That's what the man said!"

"There's a man now? How many people are you seeing in this room right now?"

"Damn it, John! I had a dream right before I saw the woman. And in the dream, the man was...he was...well, he said what you just said!"

"Hazel, for the love of God, there is no one in this room but us! Don't you think I know what goes on in my own house?"

Tears coated her cheeks again. "John, you have to let me go. I'm going to lose my mind here. You have to let me go." Her breath caught nearly every other word. He was stricken with guilt.

But his resolve was stronger. "Listen, we'll talk about this more tomorrow. For now, you need to calm down. No one is here, I promise you." He watched her collapse on the bed. She was crying so hard, he was fearful she'd wake the child. And he wasn't sure what to do if that happened.

Suddenly, there was rapid movement from behind him.

Bennings stood in the doorway holding a glass of brandy. "Will this help, sir?" John shot him a sour look, but the old man merely shrugged his shoulders. John motioned for the butler to meet him outside. As they left the room, John kept his eyes on Hazel. Tears were still running down her face, but her golden eyes were glaring at him.

He thought for a moment to just tell her the truth. Explain that Bennings had kidnapped her...well, out of the goodness of his heart. But the possibility that she wouldn't believe a word he said had John holding his tongue.

Bennings had caused this mess, but John would have to find a way to clean it up.

+++

Bennings was barely through the door to the study when John pushed it closed. He knew his employer was angry. Nothing about the situation had gone smoothly so far.

"I'm sorry, but have you forgotten that you work for me? That you do what I say?"

"Sir, I've already apologized for my actions."

"Did I ever, at any time, encourage you to kidnap someone? Did I ever ask for this?"

"I believe there is a reason I saw this woman. I believe there is a reason she hasn't truly tried to escape."

"The reason she hasn't tried to escape, Bennings, is because we're about to get a foot of snow, and I threatened her like my bastard of a father—*that* is why she hasn't tried to escape. If she knew the phones were back online, though, don't doubt for a second she'd call the police. Hell, maybe I should call them."

"Perhaps if you charm her—"

"Charm her? Isn't that a swell idea? You're right, Bennings. I'll just ask the woman you kidnapped if she'd like to go on a date. Maybe a garden picnic in the middle of a snowstorm."

"If she is truly Alison—"

"Don't! Stop doing this, Bennings. I mean it. I'm seriously worried about your state of mind. Now I have to buy off this woman just to keep you out of jail. Do you get that, old man?"

He knew what John said was valid, but the eerie feeling that plagued him before was influencing him still. Bennings couldn't explain it, but Hazel was in the house for a reason. She had a purpose. He felt that strongly.

"You know how long I wished for Alison to come back to me. Twenty years of living in hell. And what do I have to show for it?" Bennings was relieved when John reached over and patted his shoulder. "You are beyond loyal, old man. But look what that loyalty's done to you."

"Sir, I created this chaos, not you. All I want is to give you a chance. If Miss Hazel is not who I believe her to be, then I am wrong and I should go to prison for my actions. But if I'm right, sir, then you have an opportunity waiting for you. And she's just upstairs."

"Her face, Bennings. I can't get over it." He thought he heard hope in John's words. "But I'll never survive another loss."

"You have survived such a loss before."

"It almost killed me. I won't bear that pain again."

"She's not lost, sir. She's just upstairs."

+++

John paced the hall outside the kitchen and pondered Bennings's words. What if the old man was right? Dare he hope that somehow Hazel and Alison were one and the same?

The memory of having her in his arms upstairs was tormenting him. The smell of her hair, the softness of her skin—and that voice. He'd give anything to have Hazel. He'd give anything for her to look at him like Alison had.

Jesus, what sickness did he have? Wanting a woman who looked like his dead wife? Good God, what was wrong with him?

The dreaded question continued to plague him: What if he had gotten it wrong? What if Hazel really *was* somehow Alison?

No. It couldn't be. There was the birth certificate to consider.

Bennings's wild plan was just the end ropes of both their sanities failing. Alison was dead.

But she swore not even death would keep them apart. She swore she'd never leave him. And if they were ever separated, Alison swore he only need wait for her. No force on earth could rip them apart.

For the first decade, he'd held onto that hope. Each night he paced that long hallway, lighting candles and calling to her like a man possessed. He even stood on that same window ledge that claimed her. If Bennings hadn't found him and pulled him to safety, he'd have let gravity pull him into that black water. And it would have been finished.

He fell into a deep depression and for years refused to leave the house. Only his sister and Bennings were allowed near him. Had they not stood by John, he would have likely ended up in an asylum. Or dead.

Then Laura had the idea to honor Alison's memory each year. She and Bennings slowly pulled John out of his depression and grand seclusion. And in the last five years, John had felt a renewed sense of hope and faith. He thought at first it was the yearly galas and the ever-increasing socialization Bennings had pressed upon him. But it was more than that—it was the scent of juniper that filled his room on lonely nights. It was the sudden emergence of a long-lost memory of Alison, the girl he fell in love with, standing on a balcony in London, waving at passersby below, and then knocking the floor out from under him with that first intense stare.

When he laid eyes on Hazel the first time, he'd felt that old longing again. It was more than lust. It was the familiarity of a lost love. And the need to be reunited with her—body and soul.

She had to be Alison! There was too much likeness for it all to be a coincidence. He needed to break down her barriers and somehow restore the old memories. He had to find a way.

Of course, he'd have to offer her some kind of guarantee, assurance that she wouldn't be a prisoner indefinitely. And he'd have to keep his word.

How long would it take to convince her? How long would it take to convince him to let her go?

A new plan was forming, and John knew he had to put it in motion now. And he knew, without a doubt, it would be his last chance.

+++

The lifelike doll Scotty had been playing with sat at the foot of the staircase. Bennings eyed it curiously.

The house was changing. In the decades since Alison's death, John's crazed obsession with finding her again had plunged the house into darkness. With Hazel's arrival, something was happening.

The humming he heard inside the walls of the great house, it was troubling. Bennings had thought the darkest days were behind John. Now he wasn't sure.

He picked up the doll and examined it. It was curious. He had ordered all the toys for the nursery at the gala, but this peculiar doll wasn't familiar at all.

He walked slowly up the stairs and into Hazel's bedroom. Neither Hazel nor the little girl noticed him. He laid the doll on a chair near the bed and left as soundlessly as he'd entered.

He was a guilty man to execute such a loathsome plan. Hazel Loveless was an innocent woman—an innocent woman who greatly resembled the late Mrs. Stonem. If he had kept his mouth shut about seeing her, she would still be safely at home with her child.

But in the two days she had been in the house, John had come alive again. His energy, his spirit—he was a man rejuvenated.

The old butler sighed. Come hell or high water, Bennings would continue with the plan. Something was changing inside of the house. He was sure that it was all connected to Hazel.

Chapter Twelve

"I have a proposal for you."

John watched as Hazel shuffled around what looked like notebook paper inside her purse. Her hair was tied up in a bun. She wore a plain blue dress and her knees were still bruised from the accident, but he thought she looked absolutely beautiful.

"I don't think I want to hear any proposal from you." Her tone was icy and she kept her gaze on all that paper, refusing to even glance his way.

"It's not that kind of proposal." He sat down calmly in a chair and waited.

When she finally turned around to face him, he saw that her hands were clenched tightly, as if at any moment they might engage in combat.

"Alright, John. I can see you're settled in here. What is it that you want?"

"Your trust."

"Ha. I'd say you've basically blown any chance of getting that."

"Then let me make it up to you."

"And how, Mr. Stonem, do you intend to do that? Because I can only think of one way: letting me and my child leave this place unharmed."

"That's exactly what I intend to do."

He watched as she unclenched both her fists.

"What did you say?"

"I'm going to let you go."

"Why do I sense there's a big *but* coming?"

"I want to make a deal with you, Hazel."

She was smirking at him. "Oh, I get it. You'll let us go, but only if I don't go to the police."

"Not exactly." He reached in his pocket and pulled out a folded piece of paper. "This is yours."

He watched her expression as she plucked the paper out of his hand and unfolded it. It was a check made out to her. A check for $250,000.

+++

"You're joking. Guilt money?"

"No. It's yours. Look at the date."

It read a month from that day.

"What is this? Time for you to get away in case I do call the police?"

"No. It's the date you leave here."

She stared again at the check.

"I want you to stay with me for a month. Exactly a month. You and Scotty."

She faced him dead-on now. "Why?"

"I'm asking for a month of your time, and no more. In a month, you and Scotty are free to go. And as soon as you leave, you'll have this money to start over wherever you want."

Her mouth was gaping open in astonishment. "I have a job here."

"Had."

"What?"

"I have to confess that I hacked into your computer and sent in your resignation the morning after the accident."

"What?"

"I also emailed your mother and told her you and Scotty had to go away on business. She replied this morning chastising you for not calling, but looking forward to a nice visit upon your return."

"John! You ass!"

"But I'm being honest with you now."

"Are you?" Her eyes revealed mistrust. And pain.

"I'm only asking for a month."

"And what exactly do you think you will accomplish in a month's time? Am I supposed to fawn all over you? Forget that I had a life, a job, a mother?"

"It's only a month, Hazel. And you'll be well compensated for it."

She was nodding her head in disbelief. "I don't get it. What do you get out of all this? What exactly are you after?"

"I want to know you. All of you."

She scoffed coldly. "And what will happen if I refuse your request? What happens if I tell you I want to leave now?"

He shrugged and sat back in the chair. "Then you'll have robbed your child of a far better future than you yourself could provide her."

"Why? Because I'm a single mother?" Her tone was raw; he had evidently struck a nerve with that remark.

"No, your mothering skills are unquestionable. I could simply add a quarter of a million dollars to your corner."

He saw her struggle. She was conflicted.

"And there wouldn't be anything physical?"

"Not unless both parties agreed on it."

"And then Scotty and I could leave?"

"Yes, a month from today. Unless you prefer to stay longer. Or indefinitely."

She shot him a look from hell. "I need some time to think about this."

"I'll give you an hour."

"An hour!"

"This isn't *Survivor*. I'm just asking you to stay here for a month. After which time, you and your daughter leave with this check."

"And if I leave beforehand?"

His heart was pounding, but he shrugged at her question. "I'll cancel the check. But I won't harm you or the girl."

She sat on the bed, staring at the floor.

"I'll be back in an hour for your answer. You'll have freedom to roam any room in the house, as well as the garden."

The door was shut before she could respond.

+++

Freedom. The word seemed ludicrous to her.

Her thoughts returned to John's words…and the check she had crammed in her pocket.

A quarter of a million dollars for a month.

Why was she even considering this? Her mother must be worried sick! And, surely, even the few friends she had were confused and concerned.

The clock was ticking. It was ticking for her. For Scotty. For their futures. And for John's return.

That much money *would* buy a new future for Scotty. Hazel couldn't fool herself there. Years of struggling could be immediately eased. John said he would keep his word, and for some reason, she believed him. They would leave a month from today.

She glanced at her watch. John would be back soon for her answer.

She feared him. She feared what he would do if she said no.

She feared what he would do if she said yes.

Thoughts of her child made her heart hurt even more. How could she rob her little girl of such a privileged future?

But if John was lying…

She sat in the chair and scribbled in her notepad. Her decision would come at a heavy price either way.

Eyes clouded in sadness. Behind them black waters stir.

Hers was a face of love and laughter. Now what's left is a stranger's lost glare.

Where did she go when she flew away?

Chapter Thirteen

Her agreement had been plagued with guilt and doubt. John knew
that. But she *had* agreed. And he was not going to waste any time.

At dawn, he pulled back her curtains, flooding the room with
light.

"What are you doing, John?"

"I want you to go outside with me."

"Scotty's not even awake yet."

He turned to see the small sleeper next to Hazel.

"She has her own room, Hazel."

"Do you blame me for wanting to keep her close?"

"Touché."

"What do you want, John?"

"I want us to go for a walk. Together."

He smiled as Hazel begrudgingly pulled herself out of bed.

"Bennings will get Scotty her breakfast."

"Fine."

He ignored her poor attitude. "This way."

+++

Hazel followed John down a spiral staircase that was hidden
behind a rug in the hallway.

She was shocked. "How many more of these passages are
hidden behind rugs?"

He didn't answer.

The windy staircase eventually led to the back of the house.
There was a simple room with hooks—hooks that held dangling keys.
Then a series of shelves that housed baking tools. Blenders, mixers,
roasters, old convection ovens. Beside the shelving was an array of
aprons.

"What is all this?"

"Staff equipment."

"Staff?"

"You don't think Bennings cleans this whole place all by
himself?"

"But I've not seen anyone apart from you and Bennings."

"I sent them on holiday. Bennings is probably still cursing me." Hazel was surprised to hear John chuckle to himself.

He opened the back door, which led to a large veranda overlooking a garden. Much of it was covered. Frost had already been blessing the mornings.

"Beautiful, isn't it?"

It was. Blues, oranges, reds, pinks, and purples glistened. Dark shrubs pressed against pastel flowers that refused to die too quickly. It was as if autumn itself had been birthed in this garden. Everything, even the path, which seemed to be man-made of pebbles and granite, was to her taste. Trellises embraced by vines outlined every turn of the path.

It was odd. As a child, she had fantasized about having a garden of her own. A house of her own. A life of riches. And John Stonem was giving her access to his for a month. She didn't want to admit that she liked it, but she did.

"My wife designed this."

"Alison?"

Even saying the woman's name felt strange. Hazel was terribly afraid she was buying into his fantasies by even mentioning her.

"She loved the outdoors. She spent every waking moment out here. Every ounce of her energy went into perfecting this. She even helped lay the granite pathway we're standing on with her own bare hands."

"It is very beautiful."

"It could be yours, Hazel, if you want it."

"For a month, you mean?"

"For as long as you want, if I'm honest."

She grew nervous but kept her tone even. "That wasn't the deal we made, John."

"I'm not backing out of that deal. I'm merely suggesting that it doesn't have to end in a month. You could stay here, or come back here."

"I think it might be time for us to go back inside."

"Wait here for just a moment." She watched as he skipped down the pathway and out of sight.

The wind picked up, and a cool gust blasted her face. She turned away from the path and stared back at the house. On top of the veranda, she saw movement.

"John?" she called.

There was no answer, but she was sure someone was there.

"Are you up there, John? It's getting cold. Let's go back inside."

Still no answer.

She began to slowly approach the veranda. But then there was a heaviness in the air. Heaviness that made her queasy. As she rounded the path toward the steps of the veranda, a horrific sight froze her in place.

The gaunt figure of a woman stood at the top of the steps. Her back was toward Hazel. Her long, stringy hair blew sideways in the wind. Hazel felt the bile rising in her throat, and she knew the chilling vision she saw was the woman from her bedroom.

Hazel was mouthing John's name. It was the only attempt she made to save herself.

The wind picked up again. This time she saw the woman's arm rise up. One long finger pointed straight ahead—straight toward that black water.

An urgent whisper brought Hazel to her knees.

"Save them."

The roar of the water from the river bellowed inside her eardrums.

The woman slowly lowered her arm. Hazel was completely frozen in fear.

Then, to her horror, the woman began stepping backwards down the stairs. One long leg jaggedly descended; the other followed. From the way one of her legs was bent, Hazel thought it must be broken. The woman's head was slowly twitching from side to side. And the arm that had pointed to the river was now twisted and contorting behind her back—contorting in such a way that surely all the bones in that arm were broken as well. The very sight of the woman's painful movement made Hazel want to vomit.

Then that same long and skinny finger was pointing right at Hazel.

She closed her eyes so she didn't have to see any more. As she shut them tightly, her head felt heavy. Darkness clouded her mind. It was all too much—too frightening and too real. She cried out just once and felt her body falling backwards. She forgot about the garden. She forgot about the flowers. All she could think about was that black water devouring her.

+++

Bennings was boiling water for tea as John pressed a cold rag to Hazel's forehead.

"Where's the girl?"

"She's watching a television program in the study, sir."

"I don't understand what happened. I left her alone for only a moment."

John had gone to fetch a bundle of lavender for Hazel—likely the last bloom since the weather was turning so cold. He heard her scream his name and ran up the pathway, only to find her unconscious on the ground.

"Should I call a doctor?"

"No, not yet."

Slowly Hazel's eyes began to open. "What happened?"

"I was about to ask you the same thing. You scared the hell out of me."

He held onto her as she sat upright. "The woman. I saw the woman again!"

"The woman? From your nightmare?"

"She was in the garden—standing on the veranda!"

John glanced at Bennings. "Are you sure we're secure here?"

The old man nodded.

"John, I know what I saw! It was the same woman who was in my room!"

"The woman who disappeared right in front of you?"

He knew she wasn't too badly injured as soon as he caught her eye-roll. "I know how I sound, but it was real."

Bennings poured tea for both of them. John did suddenly have an awful thought: What if one of Hazel's friends was stalking the property? Or even a nosy reporter from the night of the gala?

Yet he doubted both of those scenarios. He and Bennings had been so careful to make sure all of the guests had gone. And the only access point to the house was by boat since the bridge was out.

Seeing how scared Hazel was, he tried to calm her.

"Are you're sure you didn't just hit your head on something?"

"Perhaps a concussion from the accident, sir?"

"Bennings, I hadn't even thought of that."

"No, both of you. Listen to me. It was a woman! I'm sure of it!"

John rubbed his temples. "Okay, tell me what she looked like."

"Well, I didn't see her face."

"But you know it was a woman?" He was trying not to sound annoyed.

"She had a dark gown on. And she had long hair. And a long finger."

He cocked his eyebrows. "She only had one finger?"

"No, John! I just saw one finger—she was pointing toward the river. And then at me. And she moved like she was possessed. I've never been so scared in my life!"

"Hazel! It's alright!" He was afraid her babbling was bordering on hysteria again.

He grabbed a coat from behind the kitchen chair and marched into the hallway. From the locked safe outside of the study, he grabbed a rifle.

"What are you doing?" She had followed behind him.

"I'm going to make sure we don't have some prowler lurking around the property."

"Why don't you just call the police?" He rolled his eyes at her suggestion. "At least let me go with you!"

"Unlikely! I left you for barely a minute and look what happened."

"But John!"

He held his hand up to her protests. "Bennings, make sure all the doors and windows are locked except this one." He paused before leaving. "Hazel, the woman you saw—could you make out any of her face?" A thought entered his mind.

"No, John. I didn't see it."

"So she didn't look like—" He didn't even want to form the question. "You didn't see her face then?"

"No."

He stepped outside. The wind was picking up. It was just a brief walk to the spot where he'd found Hazel. A sense of urgency quickened his senses, as if he would see something, or someone, if he were only fast enough.

He stopped when he reached the veranda. The silence was deafening. Not even the roaring river cut through the eeriness. The sunset faded away. Darkness enveloped him.

"What the hell is happening to me?" he whispered. "Hazel's nightmare…it must be affecting me."

The stillness remained—so did his sense of unease. He felt like he was supposed to see something, as if someone were holding him in that spot.

It was a ludicrous leap of faith.

"Alison?" he whispered. "If you're here, give me a sign."

He waited for any sign—a flash of light, a sound, anything.

There was nothing.

His mind returned to the last time he was with Alison.

The candles were lit near the bed. John knelt down next to Alison, whose deep breathing was audible. He traced an index finger across her lips until her eyes fluttered open.

"My plane leaves in two hours. I just wanted to say good-bye."

She nodded silently, still half asleep.

"Will you be this beautiful when I get back?" He was toying with the buttons on her nightgown.

"I'll be naked in bed waiting for you," she teased.

He cupped her face and kissed her deeply.

"I'm sending Bennings on some errands. He'll be back late tomorrow afternoon. Will you be okay here on your own?"

She was twisting her fingers around his tie. "Now, now, my darling. I won't be entirely on my own."

He rolled his eyes. "I'll tell Laura to give you some space. Better yet, I'll send her on a trip."

He watched as Alison's eyes lit up. "Oh? A lengthy trip?"

He moaned when she bit his lower lip. "I hate it when my two favorite ladies aren't getting along."

"Johnny, she's your sister but does she always have to hover around you? And Bennings caught her pocketing silver earlier. He was too uncomfortable to tell you himself."

"God, I suspected as much. She's been buying more and more crap and hasn't asked for a penny." He hated that Laura preferred to steal rather than come to him for money. Before James had thrown Laura out, Alison had caught her stealing from James's safe. Laura had run crying to John, feigning innocence. "Maybe she'd like a lengthy cruise in the Caribbean."

"The Caribbean? After your parents exiled her for all those years? I don't think so."

89

"I'll find a better place for her, and maybe have a talk with her about the stealing."

He kept examining his wife's face. She had been so upset after the fundraiser—because of his drinking. And now she was so relaxed. So loving again. "Perhaps it wasn't wise to let her move in here. Maybe James was right. I hate the lying and the stealing."

"It's not just the stealing, John. It's her constant...presence."

"Listen, my love. I'll handle Laura. I just want to make sure I'm not leaving you feeling alone and isolated here." He kissed her forehead and eyed his watch.

"Isolated? This is my sanctuary. Besides, I've decided I'd rather be here than sitting in some luxurious hotel room for a week while you're in meetings trying to save all those widows and orphans." She kissed him again, and he moaned in delight when her fingers dropped to the zipper of his trousers.

"You're going to be late, darling."

"Tease!" he stammered, and then climbed onto the bed, pinning her beneath him.

"John! You'll miss the plane!"

He grinned wickedly as he pushed up her nightgown. "Fuck the plane. I'll catch the next one."

Her laugh echoed in his mind. But he was firmly back in the present.

He was expecting to be hit with the torturous blast of grief that came whenever he thought of her. Only this time, that awful emptiness didn't come. This time, John looked back toward the house—toward the lights in the windows and the smoke slowly easing out of the chimney.

There was life.

John inhaled the cold air. The freshness soared through him as if he'd been holding his breath for twenty years.

"Alison's not dead. She's not. She's somehow been reborn in Hazel." He smiled and began walking back to the house.

If Alison's vow to never leave him was true, then Hazel *must* be the answer. Hazel *must* be Alison. Or it was all a lie. And Alison really was gone for good.

Alright then, if Hazel remembered anything about being Alison, she wasn't letting on. He hadn't noticed any odd behavior short of her nightmares and the fainting spell earlier—both of which he attributed to the current awful situation.

If John was wrong about Hazel, Bennings had indeed kidnapped an innocent woman and her child. Hazel would be right—John would be paying her off at the end of the month. But her face, oh God, her face! How could she look so much like Alison and *not* be her? He just had to make her remember.

+++

Hazel stood in the hallway near the study. Her eyes were half on Scotty and half on the door John had exited from. Upstairs, she could hear Bennings checking locks. For an old man, he worked fast.

Hours passed. John still wasn't back.

At dusk, Hazel carried Scotty up to her room. She tucked the child in, and went to peer out the window. There was no sign of John, no sign of anything.

She was careful to leave the door open in case Scotty woke up and needed her. As she walked down the hallway, she looked up at all the rugs hanging along the wall. And the drapes covering mirrors and photos.

The edge of a portrait was peeping out one side of the drapery. She pushed the cloth out of the way. There was no mystery who the woman was. Auburn hair, ruby lips, rosy cheeks. She had a dimple on her left cheek, just as did Hazel. The smile Alison wore wasn't warm or inviting, though. She seemed to be mocking Hazel. Mocking Hazel's attempt to live in *her* house, and charm *her* husband, and wear *her* clothes.

It was all fake. It was all wrong.

A sickening feeling flooded Hazel. How could she do this? Live with John for a month, listen to him talk about Alison, and know he was fantasizing that Hazel was his lost wife?

"She was a lovely woman."

Bennings's words made her jump. "I didn't hear you."

"I didn't want to wake the child."

She pointed at the photo. "She did a number on John."

He nodded. "She still does."

The solemnity in his tone gave her dread. "He refuses to just get over her? Even after all these years?"

"It's hard to get over a lost love. Harder still with Alison. She swore if they were ever separated, she'd find a way back to him. She swore all he had to do was watch for her."

The very notion made her angry. "So she essentially made him promise to always wait for her?"

"And he has."

"What a selfish bitch."

"Have you never been in love, Miss Hazel?"

She scoffed at him. "You think I'm harsh to judge her? But don't you think if she truly loved him, she'd let him go? Let him live his life happily, instead of pining away for her forever?"

"Who can say what is in Mr. John's heart? He loved her deeply. Still does."

"Is it love to be chained to a dead woman?"

"Aw, but you forget, Miss Hazel, that John has never thought of her as truly dead."

She faced Bennings and tried to be as clear as absolutely possible. "I'm *not* her, Bennings. I don't want to exacerbate any fantasies John may have. I don't want you to either. I don't want him hurt."

She flinched when Bennings reached up and patted her cheek gently. "I know you don't, Miss Hazel."

She pulled the drapery back over the portrait.

"You aren't here to deal with this, blessed Alison. You've left it to us to deal with what you've left behind." Anger swelled up inside. Some of it was rational; some of it was not. And to make the situation all the more confusing, she felt a strong pang of guilt. After all, she would be leaving the house in less than a month, and as a wealthy woman.

And she would be alive.

John would still be mourning a woman who had been in a grave for two decades.

Chapter Fourteen

A knock against her wall brought Hazel to her feet. She had been reading next to her bedroom window—and waiting, she supposed, for John to come back.

At nearly midnight, the abrupt thud sent her book to the floor and her instincts on high alert. She pressed her ear to the wall. There was another thud, and then a sigh.

She crept to her door and peered down the hallway. A lengthy rug hung on the wall between her door and Scotty's. It had perplexed her from the first day she had been here. After John took her downstairs through that hidden spiral staircase, she had a suspicion there were many more passageways. Her eyes focused in on the rug again. There had to be a door there. No surprise: When she pushed the rug away, there *was* a door. She put her hand to the knob and turned, but it was locked.

Inside her room, she pressed her ear against the wall again but heard nothing. All around the room were rugs. Damn! What if there were view holes in those rugs? Was she being watched?

She walked to the rug near the door and pulled it away from the wall. Nothing but faded wallpaper was behind it. She went to the next one, jerking the dark green print nearly off its post. But again, just faded wallpaper.

She walked to the third—an orange and gold tapestry—and pulled it away. A door was behind it, and the latch was loose. With ease, she pushed it open.

The room beyond was lit softly from a fireplace. A large bed with bronze ornaments was in the center. On the whole, the room was sparsely furnished.

She walked toward the bed. And she saw him.

He had stripped down to his boxers and was lying on top of the thick blue comforter. For the first time, she could really look at John without feeling like he was scrutinizing her.

His biceps were large and shapely, as she remembered. His chest and abdomen were sculpted—she hadn't expected that. But his face was coated with a salt and pepper beard. And his hair hung too low to his eyes.

She thought back to the night of the gala, when she had seen him talking and dancing with other women. She'd thought then that with his masculine beauty, he should have been a model. She'd wished he had turned his attention to her and maybe shared a dance.

But that was before. Before he had lied to her. Before he had orchestrated her kidnapping.

She watched silently as his chest rose and fell with each deep breath. He suddenly looked so vulnerable. As the fire began to die down, she saw him squirm. She pulled an afghan off the chair near his desk and covered him with it.

"Alison," he muttered.

"Shhh," she whispered.

"How could you leave me? Do you know what I've done?"

She stroked his hair and he quieted once more. But her heart was beating so loudly, she was scared it would wake him. His words—they stung her.

"Yes, she did a number on you. And now we're all paying the price."

She waited a few minutes to make sure he didn't awaken, and then retreated back to her room.

After closing the door between them, she sat staring out the window. Her heart hurt for him, even though she should hate him for what he had done to her and Scotty. She *did* hate him. At least, she thought she did. Yet, he had a gentle way and a protectiveness that was alien to her.

Hazel had always been on her own. And when Scotty came, it was just she and the baby. She was determined to teach Scotty to be independent and to make better choices than she herself had made.

What was she teaching Scotty now by staying? How would her little girl make sense of these strange days in the years to come?

John's sudden vulnerability reminded her of the importance of compassion. But the way he managed to enrage her to the point of murder one moment and break her heart the next was damned frustrating.

She would stay the rest of the month. She would see this through for a better future. And perhaps there was a small chance she could help John, too. She could help him see that it was finally time to move on.

Chapter Fifteen

Hazel was storming the house looking for Scotty.

"I can't believe I listened to his bullshit. I can't believe it!" She stomped into the kitchen. Bennings was scrambling eggs and making coffee. "Where is she, Bennings? Where did John hide her?"

"Miss?"

"Bennings, I'm not playing around! I've searched her room. I've searched every goddamn floor!"

"Miss Hazel, Mr. Stonem is outside playing a game with Scotty." The old man pointed to the window.

She pushed it open and a gust of cold air rushed past her.

"It snowed last night. I believe they are having a snowball fight."

She stared at the shocking sight of her daughter. Scotty was laughing with John chasing her close behind.

Judging by his coat, John had been pelted the most. Flakes of white covered most of his chest. He ran after Scotty as she giggled and squealed.

"Had enough yet? Or has my snowball mastery only challenged you more!"

Scotty squealed again in response. "I'm a better snow thrower-er than you!" With that, she chucked another snowball at him. It barely hit him, but he fell to the ground dramatically, as if critically wounded.

Hazel watched as Scotty snuck up to check on John's condition. She screamed as he grabbed her and plopped her on top of a huge snow pile. But the scream turned into a roaring laugh.

John's eyes glanced to the window, and he waved and gave Hazel a warm smile.

Scotty looked as well. "Hi, Mommy!" she squealed breathlessly.

Hazel waved back. Relief and irritation hit her gut. "How long have they been outside?"

She turned and watched as Bennings plopped four pieces of toast in the toaster, and then resumed scrambling the eggs.

"About an hour, Miss Hazel. I'll call them in when these eggs are finished."

"I wish he would have asked me," she muttered.

"I believe your daughter tore through the hallway very early and awoke Mr. John. She was begging to go outside in the snow. I am truly sorry. I saw no harm or ill intent, so I decided not to wake you."

She suddenly remembered John's outing the night before. "I don't suppose John found any prowlers?"

"He returned very late, but said he could find no one."

"So I'm going crazy."

She watched Bennings turn down the gas on the stove. He poured her a cup of coffee and ushered her into a seat at the small kitchen table. To her surprise, he sat down beside her.

"I don't think you're crazy." He glanced rather pensively at the window as John was lifting Scotty in the air and making airplane noises. "I have been in this house with Mr. John for a very long time. I worked for his parents first and knew Mr. John as a boy. When his wife died, his parents showed no concern. So I decided it would be best to stay on with Mr. John. I've never regretted that decision, but staying in this house with so much loss…it's certainly taken a toll."

"I can imagine." Indeed, if barely a week had her hallucinating, what could decades trapped inside the house manifest?

"Sometimes, when I'm alone on a floor, I think I see things that are out of order."

She calmly sipped her coffee though the atmosphere in the kitchen had suddenly changed. "Out of order? What do you mean, Bennings?"

"It is just as I said. Sometimes I think I see things that do not belong in this world." He paused as he picked up Scotty's doll from the floor and carefully placed it on another chair at the table.

"You mean a ghost? You see ghosts here?" As soon as she voiced the words, a chill swept over her. "I've never believed in ghosts, Bennings. When we die, we die."

"I never believed in ghosts either, Miss Hazel. Until two decades ago."

A frightful thought entered Hazel's mind. The woman she was seeing—what if it was Alison Stonem? "John's never mentioned ghosts, Bennings."

"I do not believe Mr. John has ever seen anything out of place. But I do believe he has wished to see something for many years."

"What have you seen, Bennings?" She nodded politely at his offer to pour more coffee into her mug.

"As I said, Miss Hazel, it was something that no longer has a place here. And that's all I wish to say."

She squeezed Bennings's hand gently. "Have you told John any of this?"

"No, Miss Hazel. I do not wish to cause Mr. John any more pain. Or false hope." Their eyes met, and Hazel's arm was covered in goose bumps as the old man squeezed her hand tightly. "And I do not wish for anyone else to say anything to Mr. John that may cause pain or give false hope."

She understood his meaning. "I won't say anything, Bennings. I'm not even sure if what I saw was real. And anyway, I won't be the cause of any more pain to John."

"Thank you, Miss Hazel. As it is, Mr. John has been let down by so many in his life. I think he has been in mourning so long that his judgment is not as keen as it once was. The only sound thing he did was throw his sister out of the house a few years ago."

"His sister?"

"Yes. Laura Stonem Cutter. She tried to commit him five years ago."

Hazel considered this. It wasn't, in her opinion, necessarily a bad idea. "I suppose John disagreed."

"He was convinced she had other motives. Since her divorce, Laura has been dependent on her late parents' trust fund, which Mr. John still controls."

"Oh. So it wasn't out of love, but out of greed."

"Mr. John was devastated. While their parents were still alive, Laura stood by him in his grief—despite their disapproval."

"John's parents were not Alison fans?"

The old man's chuckle lightened the atmosphere considerably, which relieved Hazel. "They were very traditional, very conservative. Alison believed in magic and love above all else. Mr. John was to go to Oxford and become a great businessman like his father. He was temporarily disinherited after marrying Alison against his father's wishes. Alison's influence proved to be stronger. After marrying, they traveled the world and Mr. John took jobs here and there to pay their way.

"It wasn't until after they returned from their extended honeymoon that his trust was reinstated. Mr. John had made important international connections during his excursion. People couldn't believe such a rich man would be willing to wait tables and scrub floors for the woman he loved, and to show the woman he loved the world. He came back to this country not only married, but with dozens of rich wives wagging their tails in love."

"Wow." Hazel could barely process all of it. Never in the months she lived with Duncan had she felt that kind of love and affection. A tinge of jealousy struck Hazel. It wasn't as though she thought Duncan was the love of her life, but she did ache to feel *some* kind of love with *someone*. The idea of a man like John giving up everything for one woman—she just couldn't believe such a man existed. "He loved her that much?"

"And still does."

Hazel crossed her arms. "Scotty's father never bothered to even see her when she was born."

"He tricked you, Miss Hazel? Into an unfortunate situation?"

She smiled at hearing the compassion in his voice. "I made poor decisions. Well, the wrong decisions with the wrong people. Scotty is the only thing I don't regret. I mean, my God, I'm staying here for a month in exchange for a better future for her."

"You're doing more than that, my dear." She looked into Bennings's eyes. "You're doing much more than you think." She heard the click of the stove being turned off. "I better call them inside for breakfast before it gets cold."

+++

Bennings started fixing plates. He wondered if he'd disclosed too much information to Hazel. Or perhaps not enough. It gutted him knowing she blamed John for the situation she and the child were in. Yet he hardly knew a solution—not when everything inside of him was screaming that Hazel *must* stay.

He watched as Hazel helped pull Scotty out of the snowsuit she was buckled tightly into. John pulled off his coat and kicked off his shoes. He nodded politely to Bennings before sitting down.

"Fresh coffee, sir."

Bennings watched in astonishment as John poured a touch of creamer into the mug. It was a simple change in routine. No one would have noticed it except Bennings. Yet for so long, the coffee was black. The eggs were over-easy. The toast was dry. Life was sour.

Hazel arrived and suddenly the windows were bleeding in more sun. Even the light in the hallways was brighter. There was jam on the table, butter and cinnamon on the toast.

But there was something just under the surface of that newfound sweetness that Bennings experienced. There was someone he swore he saw but couldn't possibly have seen. *She* was just a shadow. Just a remnant of the past. At least, that's what Bennings told himself.

But by her own words, Hazel was sensing something, too. It was as if the past was reawakening. Was Hazel the key to it all?

He watched as Scotty climbed into her chair. She had her doll sitting beside her. The doll Bennings had found at the foot of the stairs. For some reason, the girl took to it more than any other toy.

He didn't like that doll. It was a peculiar item to dislike, but its very presence made him uneasy. Blonde hair, blue eyes, and an extra-wide smile. It was another misleading thing—something that at surface level looked fine and normal. As he stared harder at the doll, he could have sworn the damned thing winked at him.

He looked at both John and Hazel. Neither appeared to have seen it.

"Everything alright, Bennings?" He saw John's concerned expression.

He shook his head. "Yes, sir. Only daydreaming. I apologize." He poured more coffee into Hazel's cup.

Either he was finally losing his grip, or something *was* truly happening to him—to all of them.

+++

Hazel ate in silence, observing John and Scotty. He carved eyes into Scotty's toast with a butter knife and shoved pieces of egg inside each hole. In return, Scotty rearranged John's eggs into a smiley face.

The sentiment warmed her heart but also hurt her. Scotty should have a father. Scotty deserved a father. How could she have been so irresponsible as to sleep with Duncan?

A raw memory echoed in her mind—her mother's words scorched her with their accuracy.

"Hazel, what's wrong with you? Where did my sunshine girl go? You were supposed to make better decisions than me. And here you are, right where I was once."

Hazel thought about her childhood. Her earliest memory was waking up in a hospital surrounded by strange faces. Her room in Beth's apartment was full of dolls that were alien to her. For most of her life, she felt displaced.

Beth was a career waitress, and when Hazel turned sixteen, she got a waitressing job at a diner just across the street from where her mother worked. It seemed like the most natural thing. But her mother wanted better. She wanted Hazel to dance or at least go to college. She wanted Hazel to find a nice man to fall in love with, marry, have a child with.

Hazel could never quite find her footing anywhere. She worked one menial job after another. She had one or two boyfriends before making the mistake of dating Duncan. At twenty-two, she was alone and pregnant. And like Hazel, Scotty would grow up never knowing her father.

Now here she sat—in the house of her kidnapper, who was playing the role of father to her child.

"Hazel? Are you alright?" John's question brought Hazel back to the present. She nodded to him, and he returned to the game of breakfast once more.

After finishing up, Scotty was adamant she help Bennings with the laundry. Hazel smiled warmly at the old man. He'd taught the girl a little laundry rhyme, and she was giddy to assist in what she surely didn't consider a chore.

"Colors on the left and whites on the right. Detergent on top and the lid nice and tight." She sang along and sorted while Bennings measured out detergent. It warmed Hazel's heart hearing her little girl sing and laugh so heartily.

It also frightened her.

Feeling confused, Hazel headed out into the garden, choosing to forget about yesterday's encounter with that ghoulish woman. The need for solace overtook her fear. She longed for just one quiet moment to herself.

She wandered under a trellis and found an oval bench. She brushed the snow off of it and noticed the tips of some frozen blue flowers standing up from the ground. Beyond that, she could see the river and hear the water slapping gently against the bank below. The air smelled heavenly. It was strange that the water seemed so menacing from upstairs, and now, so calm and tranquil.

"I didn't expect to find you here after what happened yesterday."

John's voice didn't alarm her. In fact, she figured he'd make his way to her. He always did.

"Is Scotty still tormenting Bennings?"

She felt the bench shift as he sat down beside her. "I think he is very taken with her. It's been a long time since there's been laughter in the house."

She looked over at him. He suddenly seemed grim. "Has something happened?"

"No. You're still here, and for that, I'm very grateful."

A pang of guilt hit her. She was staying, of course, for the money. "Did you need something, John?"

When he looked at her, she wanted to die. So much loneliness and despair. Then, in a single breath, that pained look vanished and he was smiling at her warmly. "Bennings told me you never married Scotty's father."

Oh, here we go. "No, he split."

"I'm sorry. I don't understand that type of man."

She smirked. "There are many men who walk away. That's the easier path. Parenting a child is not easy. I spend so much time worrying about getting food on the table, getting bills paid, and of course, making sure she's safe. All the while, I get to hear my mother's lecture about making the same mistakes she did."

"Your mother—you're close?"

"Oh, God, we fight like hell. She's perpetually angry with me."

"Angry with you?"

Hazel laughed lightly, without humor. "I was in an accident when I was just a little older than Scotty is now. I was in a coma for two months. When I woke up, I couldn't remember anything. Well, I still can't remember anything."

John cocked his eyebrow at her statement. "What kind of accident were you in?"

"I was electrocuted."

"Electrocuted? Dear God!"

She chuckled again. "Don't worry. It's not as dramatic as it sounds. I don't remember anything, but apparently a utility company was doing an emergency repair. There was a live wire just lying there on the sidewalk where I was riding my bike. I wasn't paying attention. And *zap*."

She thought his eyes were going to jump right out of their sockets. "God! The workers should have been more careful! That's terrible."

"Well, it's terrible for Beth Loveless. I have no memory of it. I just woke up one day confused and…I don't know…"

"Lost?" he answered for her.

"Yes, actually."

"How old were you when this happened?"

"I was six. It was the day before Thanksgiving."

He made a strangled noise that she couldn't comprehend. "Are you okay, John?"

"Yes, I'm fine. I'm glad you're alright now."

"Yeah, I'm fine. Scotty's fine. But my mother is still angry that I took Scotty when I moved to St. Jerome."

He put his hand on top of hers, and she didn't shove it away. In fact, she found herself liking the gesture.

"I often wonder what it would have been like if Alison and I could have had a child. I can think of nothing more gratifying than having a child with the woman I love. Watching her grow. Knowing she's a living legacy of our love. Proof that there's more to life than money and power." He stroked her hand gently, and then removed his own. Hazel was disappointed at his withdrawal. "I guess that's why I feel such disdain for men like that."

"I'm sorry you never had a child," Hazel added softly. "I'm sure you'd make a wonderful father."

He looked out to the river. "I very much enjoy having Scotty here, sincerely. I hope you know that."

She wasn't sure what to say. The confusion she felt hadn't exactly dissipated. So instead, she changed the topic. "Bennings told me about your sister." She could have sworn he flinched. "I'm sorry if that was a secret."

+++

John waited a moment before responding. He kept his gaze focused on the river. "Laura is planning on visiting next weekend. I was hoping to put her off, but in truth, I haven't seen her in a couple years. And despite her many, many faults, I do sort of miss her."

"What's she like?"

He sighed. Explaining Laura wasn't exactly easy. "I suppose Bennings told you she tried to have me committed?"

"He mentioned it."

"Laura is my only sibling. She's just a couple years younger than me, but was born with all kinds of respiratory problems. My parents sent her away for several years without visiting while she recuperated, which is partly why her adult life has been so eventful." *Partly.*

"Being sick and away from home and family—that must have been difficult."

"Even though our parents have been dead the last fifteen years, I doubt she's ever forgiven them."

"Bennings said she was divorced."

"Yes. Thank God. It's the only smart thing she ever did."

"What was the guy like?"

"Cutter was a gold-digging drifter. The marriage only lasted nine months and it ended nearly a decade ago. Why she still uses his name is beyond me."

Her laughter warmed his heart. "Maybe she liked the looks of him."

"Dark hair, light eyes, and a weird beard. Oh, and at the core, a true bastard."

"Well, that could be describing *you* under the right circumstances."

He smirked. "Touché. But I used to be clean shaven…and charming."

He wanted to look into her eyes. He wanted to see into her soul. The electrocution story was surprising, to say the least. Hazel's accident coincided with Alison's death. Was it just a coincidence?

He was half in a trance listening to the water, and half in a trance thinking of what a young Hazel Loveless looked like when she woke up from a coma so confused and utterly lost.

And alone. He understood that.

Then Hazel made a statement that took him completely off guard.

"You could be clean shaven again."

Her smile was warm. The fear in her eyes from the other night had vanished. And he was suddenly the terrified one. Bennings might have been right. Hazel, indeed, might be Alison, as John hoped.

But how in the world could he connect to this woman without frightening her or chasing her away?

"You aren't a fan of facial hair?" he said simply, hoping like hell she didn't hear his heart pounding against his chest.

"I guess I'd rather see the real face of the man buying my daughter a new future."

He returned her smile. He was, as she just pointed out, paying Hazel off. But she was also softening, just a little. She had opened up to him. She had revealed things about her life that he knew were unpleasant. Shouldn't he take that as a sign?

He was desperate to meet her gaze, but she seemed to purposely be looking away from him now. Perhaps she felt something as well. He hoped she did.

"It's not just Scotty's future, Hazel. I want what's best for both of you."

"This is only for a month, John." Yet he noted her voice was no more than a whisper.

"It's for as long as you want."

Chapter Sixteen

Her bedroom closet was now full of Alison Stonem's clothes. From day to eveningwear, and from simple pajamas to very revealing negligees. It seemed John had taken the lot and given it to her. That he included the negligees seemed very presumptuous to her. They had made an agreement and she certainly hadn't instigated anything.

Yet the talk in the garden had left her with a great sense of hope. Hope and security. And, if she was honest, a great deal of compassion. Maybe after all of this was over, they could even be friends; maybe they wouldn't say good-bye forever.

John hadn't instigated anything, either. In fact, he had done the opposite. He praised her child and offered a sympathetic ear. She hadn't intended on telling John about the accident. But for some reason, she needed to speak the words. She needed to confess to someone because she still felt inadequate for what she had lost. Maybe had Beth not been so open about her hurt and disappointment, Hazel could have moved on. But neither ever had. Beth was perpetually disappointed while Hazel was lost.

All Hazel wanted to do was write, but instead of going to college or even attempting to get a scholarship, she chickened out. She went from one menial job to another. And she found herself nowhere.

Only now she was in John Stonem's house. A "guest" in his house. The night of the gala, she had a strange thought her life was going to change, but she never envisioned this reality.

She shouldn't whitewash the situation. John had *kidnapped* her and Scotty—and all because she looked like Alison. John, who was attractive and wealthy and who could have any woman he wanted, had trapped her here. And worse, instead of being sickened and fleeing the house at the first opportunity, she was staying for the month. For money. For a better future. But she also didn't hate staying at the house. It was warm. Scotty was happy. They would both be secure.

John was lonely. John was hurting. Despite his supremely bad behavior and the disturbing degree of trouble he went to in securing her, Hazel was finding it harder to believe that John would hurt her or Scotty. She, on the other hand, could certainly hurt him by simply leaving at the end of the month.

While the man's troubled life tugged at her heart, she had Scotty to consider. Scotty's future would be ripe with possibilities and opportunities. She would have the life that neither Hazel nor her mother had had. Scotty would make it. And while Hazel maybe couldn't brag to the single mom's club about doing it all on her own, she was making sure that her child would not struggle. And she was doing it in a month's time.

"Mommy, look at me! I'm a lamp!"

She turned to see Scotty stomping into her bedroom with a lampshade over her head. Her arms were straight out at her sides, and she was making a roaring noise.

"Scotty, take that off your head." She pulled the lampshade off before the child could respond. "Come here, I want to talk to you."

Scotty climbed into her mother's lap. As they had done every night before John Stonem entered the picture, Hazel began to brush the little girl's hair and pull off her shoes and socks.

"I don't want to go to bed yet," Scotty whimpered.

"You aren't. We're talking first."

"Then can I have some hot cocoa?"

"Maybe later. I want to ask you something, Scotty."

"What?" Hazel stifled a giggle as the girl made faces in the mirror.

"What do you think about this place? What do you think of John and Bennings?"

"I love Benny! He's polishing a sled for me. John's taking me sledding tomorrow!"

"Oh, it's so nice how they both consulted me." She saw the puzzled expression on the girl's face. Hazel put on a bright smile for her daughter. "I guess that's very kind of them. You like John as well, then?"

"He needs to work on his snowball throwing." Hazel chuckled. "Mommy?"

"Yes?"

"How come John looks so sad?"

Hazel stroked the girl's hair. "He's been alone in this house for a long time."

"I think we make him feel better."

"I hope so."

"Mommy?"

"Yes?"

"Can we stay here?"

"We are staying here—for three more weeks, remember? Then we're leaving to see your nana."

"And John comes too, right? And then we come back here?"

"Scotty, no. It's just for three more weeks."

"But what about Benny? And John?"

"Scotty, we aren't their family."

"I want to *stay* here, Mommy. I have toys here, and a daddy."

"What?" That last word startled Hazel.

"I want John to be my daddy. He likes you, Mommy. He likes you like daddies like mommies."

Her heart was shattering. "Scotty…"

"Mommy, it's warm here. We don't have to wear two pairs of socks to bed. And John can be my daddy."

She wasn't prepared for this. She knew even this short stay could effect Scotty. And here it was—staring her right in the face. "You better put your pajamas on, baby." She turned her head to wipe tears away. In all the confusion and guilt of taking money for staying with John, she had never felt such pain as at hearing her child's plea for the most mundane of things.

Scotty didn't care about going to a fancy school or college. She didn't care about wearing clothes that didn't come from a discount store. She cared about not wearing socks to bed, staying warm, and having a father.

"Oh, my God. I'm so stupid," she murmured to herself.

Hazel tucked Scotty into bed and began reading a story to her. Luckily, the child fell asleep before the third page. Hazel suddenly wanted to lock herself away somewhere and cry. Instead, she grabbed the pen and notepad, as she had done a thousand times before.

She scribbled for pages until the thoughts could no longer be contained on mere paper. Defeated, she descended the stairs to the main floor. The study looked empty and was just feet away. She'd have her cry and figure out a way to tell John she couldn't do this anymore. She'd have to find a way to make him understand.

"Hazel?"

She turned and stared at a face she barely recognized. "John?"

John?

His beard had been shaved. His hair had been trimmed. The silver and gray that were on the sides of his head had been blended away. As if the bastard hadn't been attractive enough before.

+++

"Wh-why did you do this?"

"You said you didn't like facial hair." His smile faded when he saw the tears that were drying on her cheeks. "Hazel, what's wrong? Did you see that woman again?" He watched her as she shook her head and tried to stifle a sob. He closed the space between them and cupped her face in his hands. "Tell me what's wrong. What's got you so upset?"

"I don't know what I'm doing here." Her voice was barely a whisper.

"You're getting a better future—that's what you're doing here."

"No! I mean, I thought that at first. But now—"

"Now what?"

"I don't know what I'm doing anymore. I don't know if I'm getting a better future for Scotty or just confusing her and hurting her. I don't know if I'm leading you on. I don't know what's happening."

He led her into the study and shut the door behind them. Then he poured a glass of brandy and handed it to her. She was still trying to stifle her sobs, and that irritated him. He didn't want her to hide her emotions—even if he was the cause of them.

"Take a sip. It'll help." But he saw the tears running down her cheeks.

"I feel so lost, John. I should hate you but I don't." He took the glass from her hands and pulled her into his arms. "I should hate you for uprooting my life and creating this chaos. And for making Scotty a part of your scheme! What's wrong with me that I don't? Am I so greedy that I can explain this away to myself and my child?"

"You're right. You should hate me. For what I've done. For what I'll still do."

He felt her body stiffen in his arms. "What will you do, John? Am I going to be punished for this little outburst? Because trust me, I already feel broken!"

He seized the moment—and he seized her anguish—and kissed her. Not a mere pressing of his lips upon hers, but a thorough, passionate surge of force.

Her lips were honey. Her lips were fire. They fed his own heat—his own lost desires for the woman he was mourning. It was a strange sensation. There was a familiarity in kissing her, the familiarity that he craved. But she was also so different. Her skill, the way she let him lead the act.

Kissing her didn't *feel* like being with Alison. But it was so damn good. He could lose himself in her. He could lose himself forever.

At first Hazel had clawed her fingernails into his forearms in rebellion. But as his kiss deepened, her fingernails retracted. But she clutched onto him still. He guided her hands around his neck. He was completely at her mercy. She could strangle him, but instead she latched on.

This is what he wanted. To feel his lips on hers. To feel her arms around him. More, more, more. He wanted so much more! His hand caressed the back of her neck and his mouth continued to engage her. Her sob turned into a moan, and his entire body reacted immediately.

Kissing her was so good, but it wasn't enough. He wanted to strip her naked and explore her body. He wanted to bury himself so deeply inside her that decades of pain would be vanquished into nothingness.

He was waiting for her to push him away. He was ready for that. And he would honor and respect that. Instead, she shocked him by rubbing her hip against his strangled erection.

"Oh, God. Hazel, I want you. Tell me no now and I'll stop. Only say it now before I lose control, I'm begging you." He looked into her face—she was flushed and breathless. He thought for a moment his heart was beating so loudly that it was audible in the room. Then he realized it was someone knocking on the door.

He reluctantly let go of Hazel and approached the door. "Scotty? Did you wake up, sweetheart?" John looked back at Hazel, who was still catching her breath. She grabbed the brandy and downed half the glass quickly.

"It's Bennings, sir."

John saw what looked like relief—and embarrassment—on Hazel's face.

He opened the door. "What is it?"

"Your sister is here, sir."

+++

John closed the door to the study and walked quickly down the hall with Bennings.

"How did she get here, Bennings? Did she say?"

"She rented a boat, sir."

John didn't want to leave Hazel. In fact, what he wanted to do was give Laura a quick hug and hello and send her to a hotel. He knew better. Two years of not seeing each other—Laura wouldn't be sent away so easily. But she had arrived a week early. And he wasn't entirely sure how he was going to explain Hazel's presence, much less her face.

At the end of the hallway, he saw her. Tall, stark black hair in a tight updo. Her back was to him as she hung up her coat and scarf. Slowly, she turned around. Her sublime brown eyes grew twice as large as she opened her arms.

"John!" She embraced him warmly. He reciprocated less firmly—still mind-boggled that he had just kissed the woman he was in love with.

When Laura withdrew, he watched as she scrutinized him. Her cold hand rippled across his face, but her smile seemed to say she was pleased. "You look wonderful! No more shaggy brother. Bennings, when did you talk him into finally shedding all that hair?"

The old man said nothing.

"Bennings had nothing to do with it. I just felt it was time for a change." She stood in front of him and extended her arms in the air, and then very dramatically turned to her side. It was a game. A game she played with him when they were children, and he recognized what she wanted immediately. "Yes, Laura, you look beautiful." He smiled at her wild grin.

"Not bad for a woman pushing forty, right?" He stepped aside as she sashayed by. "I'm dying for a drink. You know, I've been traveling nonstop. Paris, Nepal, Buenos Aires, Vegas." John rolled his eyes as she rambled on. "And now I'm here—in the heart of the Midwest. My brother's land."

"Is that why you're here, Laura? Or did you run out of the settlement money I gave you?"

Without missing a beat, she said, "John, oh no. I've been running with Sebastian LePierre. He's a billionaire, you know. He owns a large percentage of wineries in Napa Valley and, well, all over!"

"I'm familiar with LePierre, Laura. He used to be a business partner, and he's notorious for picking up international call girls." His words were like ice, but the thought of Laura in the clutches of a Lothario like Sebastian made John utterly angry. "If you needed money, you should have sucked up your pride and called me."

"Called you, dear brother? After you oh-so-charmingly threw me out of this house?" He caught the crossness in her tone and matched it with his own.

"I know what LePierre is, Laura, and I don't want my sister—"

"It doesn't really matter, John. You see, Sebastian and I have decided not to see each other anymore. Probably a wise decision. All that travel was really getting to me. A girl my age has to keep her looks together before it all crumbles apart, right?"

But John knew her better than that. Likely LePierre had called off the affair. And it was lack of pride—and lack of funds—that had brought Laura back. "Dear, if you need money, just tell me how much. I'm sure I can help."

He rolled his eyes again as Laura danced around the subject, waving her hand at him like he was the servant and she the queen. "Oh, it's far too late in the evening to talk about money, don't you think? I'm dying for a strong drink, a hot bath, and you know, Bennings, some of your famous beef stew would sure hit the—"

John saw Laura's jaw drop.

"Hi there. I didn't mean to startle you." Hazel's sudden appearance made John weak in the knees. He hadn't figured the shock and awkwardness of their meeting would happen so quickly.

"Jesus Christ," Laura whispered. "Alison?"

"My name is Hazel Loveless. Your brother has been taking care of me and my daughter. We were in a car accident."

"A car accident?" Her tone was breathy, and John stood behind her in case she fainted. But his eyes focused entirely on Hazel and her nonchalant explanation. What was she doing?

"Yes, we attended the gala for Alison. The road was wet and slick and my taxi veered off the road. If John hadn't been there, well, I hate to think of what might have happened." John couldn't believe how quickly Hazel concocted her story—or comprehend why she was covering for him—unless she *was* developing feelings for him.

Judging from Laura's reaction, her story seemed to have worked. Laura relaxed and shakily offered her hand to Hazel. "I'm John's sister, Laura. I don't suppose it would come as a shock if I told you that you look exactly like—"

"—Alison Stonem? Yes, I know. It's a very strange coincidence."

"You look like an *older* version of her." John pinched his sister's arm. "Well, she does! I see a couple of eye wrinkles!"

"Well, I'm twenty-seven this coming spring. I understand Alison was in her early twenties when she died."

"Yes. A terrible accident."

"I'm sure you two would like some time alone. I'll just go check on Scotty. It was nice meeting you, Laura."

As soon as Hazel was out of sight, John felt a sharp pinch from Laura—sharper than the one he had given her. "John, what the hell is going on?"

John motioned to Bennings, and the old man thankfully knew an exit signal when he saw one. "I'll start on that beef stew, Miss Laura."

John had to hush Laura until Bennings was also out of sight. "I know what you're thinking," he began.

"A car accident? John, what did you do?"

"It's not what you think."

"That woman is a dead-ringer for your wife. An 'accident' doesn't just happen to a woman with that face." She looked devastatingly disappointed.

"I didn't hurt Hazel, or her child, if that's what you think."

"John, I was with you for years. I heard you crying out in the night for that woman. And I *know* you would do anything—anything at all—to get her back. But this is not the way."

"Laura, I didn't do anything wrong. And if I had, why in the world would Hazel be covering for me?" He was lying to his own sister. He was lying through his teeth. But Hazel *had* covered for him. And in the back of his mind, he wondered if the kiss they had shared earlier had anything to do with it.

The disapproving stare of his sister reminded him of the danger Bennings had created for them. And for Hazel. "You tricked that woman, no doubt."

"Laura, be reasonable. I will admit there is an uncanny resemblance. That's a large reason why Hazel was invited to the gala in the first place."

"And the 'car accident'? You want me to believe you had nothing to do with it?"

He could tell her the truth—he could come clean about Bennings committing a felony. But knowing Laura, she wouldn't be able to keep her mouth shut. And everything he was doing for Hazel was, in part, to protect the old man.

"Alright." John walked her into the study and closed the door. He filled another glass with brandy. He roughly placed the glass in her hand and stood with his back to her.

"I cut the brakes on the taxi."

"John!"

"There was really never any danger—Bennings was driving. The car skidded off the road and broke open the bridge, which, yes, could have ended badly, but Bennings grabbed the child and I grabbed Hazel, and everyone is just fine."

There. He'd done it. He waited for Laura's dramatic reply as she downed half the glass and then stammered. "No, John, everything is *not* fine. What if that woman finds out what you did? And the car— how are you going to get rid of the car?"

"The car went over the bridge and is now sitting at the bottom of the river."

"Christ!"

"Laura, you wanted the truth—there it is."

"What exactly are you going to do now? Keep her here in this house? Why the hell is she still here if the gala was ten days ago?"

"She's recuperating."

"And then what?"

He didn't honestly know how to answer her. So he tried a half-truth. "I wanted to make sure she wasn't Alison. She's not. She can leave whenever she would like to leave. As far as she knows, the taxi crashed and Bennings and I pulled her and her daughter out of the car. And that's all she is going to know, right? You owe me, Laura."

He saw her face twitch. "I hope you know what you're doing, John. All that woman has to do is make a call to the police—"

"She's not going to do that." And oddly, John felt sure of that. But she might if she knew about the taxi. "You owe me for the hell you put me through, Laura. You betrayed my trust."

"Yes, yes." She was clearly exasperated, but she relented. "I'm not going to say a word about this. God help you if she does find out."

"If you don't tell her, she can't possibly find out."

"John, you are such an idiot. Wasn't there a kid inside? Didn't she witness this, too? Maybe she heard something or saw something incriminating? It's obvious the mother didn't."

He hadn't thought about exactly what Scotty did or didn't remember about the crash. Laura's revelation suddenly chilled him. But if Scotty recalled that Bennings had been their driver, surely she would have told her mother by now?

Suddenly everything was hanging by the thread of a four-year-old's memory.

Chapter Seventeen

Bennings found Hazel standing alone in the kitchen. "Did you need anything, Miss Hazel?"

"Actually, I was going to ask you the same thing."

"I'm just going to start a stew for Miss Laura." He tried to hide the inflection in his voice when he said Laura's name.

"I hope I didn't make things too uncomfortable for John."

Bennings noted her concern. He liked Hazel; he felt that she genuinely cared about John's well being. Laura, on the other hand…

"I'm not really sure why I covered for him, if you want to know the truth. But her sister's very…in your face, so to speak."

"That's one way of putting it, Miss Hazel. Miss Laura has never held back."

"She seems very intense. Makes me happy to be an only child."

Bennings smiled. There were small things about Hazel that reminded him of Alison. The fact that both women took an immediate dislike to Laura didn't go unnoticed.

"I am hopeful Mr. John will be able to provide Miss Laura with what she needs so that she can take her leave."

"Do you think she's just here for the money?"

"I've never entirely understood Miss Laura's motives. I just know Mr. John is always pensive when she's here." Come to think of it, the house itself felt pensive and encumbered. As if it were objecting to Laura's arrival. But he didn't want to burden Hazel with his thoughts.

Or his guilt. He was selfishly glad Hazel was sticking around because he had grown so fond of little Scotty. The only family Bennings ever really had was John—and when Alison died, he also felt the loss. Hazel's presence had sparked life in the house again. And little Scotty's energy and laughter warmed his heart.

Perhaps, he thought, his plan to kidnap Hazel and her child wasn't all for John's benefit after all. Perhaps he was trying to restore something that had been taken from him as well.

As he examined Hazel's face more closely, it became obvious the woman had been crying. Her eyes were red and swollen, and her cheeks were pinker than normal.

"Is everything alright, Miss Hazel?"

+++

Hazel smiled—it was probably an over-the-top kind of smile—but she didn't want Bennings to know what had occurred between her and John. She could barely absorb the shock of it herself.

One minute, she was so guilt-ridden she was sure she was going to leave.

Then she was in John's arms. Then she was letting him kiss her. Worse, she was kissing him back. She was igniting his lust and nearly matching it with her own. Had Bennings not interrupted when he had, she wasn't sure how far it would have gone.

"Are you sure I can't get you anything?"

She was watching Bennings chop up thick cuts of beef. For a man clearly pushing eighty, he was far from limited in his abilities. From aiding John in whatever insane plan to cooking a midnight dinner—it was impressive. Hazel herself was growing exhausted just watching him.

"I'm alright, Bennings. It's been a long day."

"Indeed." She saw him flinch and put down his knife.

At first she thought he had cut himself, but when he bent over to pick something up off the floor, she was relieved to see nothing more than a doll.

Except Bennings looked at it strangely.

"Bennings? What's wrong?"

He handed her the doll quickly. "I thought I sent it with Miss Scotty earlier."

"Yes, this is the doll she's been glued to. I'll take it upstairs. Good night, Bennings."

Maybe in the morning she and John could talk. The day's events had left her heart quaking. She wasn't sure if it was out of apprehension…or a feeling that was so alien to her, the very thought of it frightened her.

On the way to the staircase, she spotted Scotty watching television in the study.

"It's time for bed," she called.

The little girl grinned mischievously. "Fifteen more minutes?"

She was too tired to fight even such a small battle. "Ten minutes. Then I want you upstairs."

The words Hazel had written up in her room earlier were terrible. She should rip up the pages from her notepad and throw them away forever. And yet, no matter what had transpired, she could never find it in her heart to throw her writing away. Writing was the only way her innermost thoughts and fears could be safely unleashed. Even when those thoughts and experiences were unpleasant, she still couldn't rip the pages up and throw them away. Strangely, the cheap pages of that notepad were the most precious pieces of her.

Alone in her room, she flipped through the sheets and added just one last sentence. A simple four-word sentence.

+++

John made sure Laura's bedroom was on the second floor—literally on the other side of the house from his own room. He didn't want her to know that Hazel was sleeping right next door to him. Knowing Laura, she'd find out on her own time. She'd find out everything.

There was so much on his mind. Suddenly Scotty was the tie that could bind everything together—or tear everything apart. And just when Hazel was beginning to come around to him. That kiss. That kiss had been electric. He very much wanted more than just a kiss. Had Laura not shown up when she had…

It didn't matter. At least Laura had pointed out the one vulnerability neither John nor Bennings had considered.

Suddenly he felt sick. Despicably and utterly sick. Bennings's plan had been so risky. It could have gone so very, very wrong. Hazel and Scotty could have gone over that bridge with the taxi—hell, it had almost happened! He would have held himself responsible.

"I need Mrs. Winkles."

The tiny voice behind him nearly gave him a heart attack. He turned to see Scotty standing in her pajamas looking frantic. "I looked under my bed and in my closet and she's not anywhere!"

He kneeled in front of her. The freckles on her face must have come from her father, whoever he—Duncan—was. But her eyes were her mother's. And her smile. And her frown.

"Who's Mrs. Winkles?"

She playfully bopped him in the head. "My dolly is Mrs. Winkles!"

He gazed at her, puzzled. "Why do you call her Mrs. Winkles?"

"Because that's her name!"

Fair enough.

"Where was the last place you saw Mrs. Winkles, sweetheart?"

"I don't know, but I gotta find her. She can't sleep without me."

"Maybe you left her in the kitchen." He cupped her little face, and the realization of what Bennings risked in kidnapping Hazel was painfully obvious.

"No, no, no." She tapped her tiny index finger against her temple. "Maybe she's sleeping with Mommy."

The little girl tiptoed to her mother's bedroom and knocked lightly before opening the door. John followed her into the bedroom. Hazel was reclining in a chair by the window. Moonlight lit up her face. Her eyes were closed, and her hand hung loosely from her arm.

"Mommy's sleeping," Scotty whispered.

"Yes, we shouldn't wake her." His voice was beginning to tremble. His whole world—or the world he was aching to have— was here in this one bedroom.

Then Scotty spotted her doll. It was nestled under Hazel's arm. "Mrs. Winkles *is* sleeping with Mommy!" Her whisper was a loud-pitched cry of excitement. It was enough to awaken Hazel.

Drowsily, she pulled the doll from under her arm. "Here, baby. You should be in bed." She yawned and picked up the girl, who clutched her doll.

John was sickened.

"John? Are you okay?"

Tears began to trickle down his face. He was absolutely horrified. What might Bennings have done?

"Scotty, be a good girl and go to bed now. I'll check on you later." A swift kiss on her forehead and the little girl started to dart from the room. She paused long enough to hug John's leg, and then scampered into her room.

"Did you and your sister have a fight?"

He wiped his face and turned his back toward her. "She knows me better than most."

"She didn't buy my story?"

The tenderness in her voice forced more tears. "Why did you lie, Hazel?"

She grabbed a glass of water from the end table and handed it to him. "Because deep down, I don't believe you're a terrible person, John."

He downed the water and slammed the glass back on the table. "You don't know me, Hazel. As much as I wish you did."

"I know you loved your wife—*still* love your wife. I know you'd do anything to see her again." She sat on the edge of her bed. "I sometimes feel myself getting jealous when I listen to you or Bennings talk about her. About how much you love her."

He sat down next to her. "What could you be jealous of? You've made it clear you aren't Alison and don't want to be."

+++

He sounded bitter.

"I may not be Alison, but I would love to have that kind of relationship with a man. Not the obsessively grieving and kidnapping part, of course." She stifled her own laugh. "But the consuming love part. That would have been nice. I wonder what I'll tell Scotty when she's older. I guess I could lie and tell her that Duncan and I were madly in love, but that doesn't exactly set a great precedence for love, seeing as he walked out on us."

Now *she* sounded bitter. But she still saw the worry in John's eyes.

"Maybe we've both been ruined by our partners. They both let us down terribly. And we're the ones left picking up the pieces." She wanted him to see what she saw so clearly. That Alison was hurting him as much as Duncan had hurt her—more so—as John's grief had consumed him his entire adulthood.

"No, it's not quite the same. You never loved Duncan like you thought you should have. I can hear it in your voice when you talk about him. But I *do* love Alison. She didn't let me down. She's still here." He grabbed hold of Hazel's hand and placed it against his chest. She could feel his heart beating beneath the crisp white shirt. "I can feel her here, right now."

"And does she still speak to you?"

His silence was her answer.

"My God, John. She's done such a number on you, and you don't even see it."

Suddenly his head was against hers, and he was whispering like a lost lover. "No, Hazel. I've never been blind when it came to love. I knew it as soon as I saw it. But you, you resist. You've had a life full of disappointment, and the idea of love is so alien that you reject its mere existence—except for with Scotty."

"No, that's not true."

"I *know* love. I know what's in my heart. But I also know that I can't keep going on like this. Too many lives are at stake."

She faced him, unclear at his meaning.

"I want to kiss you again."

She considered pushing him away, but that kiss they shared plagued her.

"I can't believe that kiss happened. I was so upset. You see, Scotty and—"

"And nothing. You felt something. You needed something from me. *I* felt it. That kiss did nothing but confirm what we both know."

Hazel shook her head. "This isn't love, John. This is something that I can't even give a name to."

"I might call it lust. Because I do dream of you, Hazel. I dream of you in my bed, crying out my name—"

"John!"

"You didn't think about what could have happened if Laura hadn't shown up?"

They locked eyes. Her breathing quickened. "I dream of you, always. First I dreamt of you as Alison, remembering me suddenly, reaffirming our love. But now I dream of *you*, Hazel. Scotty's mother. A woman who just showed undeserved loyalty when all I've done is stolen her world out from under her."

"I do hate you for that, John. And for the confusion Scotty is now feeling."

"I wish Scotty were mine. I wish there had never been any Duncan in your life. I cringe thinking that any man would have the nerve to make love to you and then walk away."

She was blushing. She knew she was. "But it happened, John. It happens to a lot of women. I'm really not that extraordinary." She sounded breathless.

"You, not extraordinary?" His words were roughened with passion.

"I'm just Hazel, John. There is no larger-than-life anything about me. I'm a mother. I wanted to be a writer, but all I do is scribble on a notepad. I worked a bunch of lousy diner jobs. And now, I schlep coffee for the St. Jerome paper. At least, I *did*."

"That's far from the truth, which you continue to shield from everyone. Tell me what you write about."

"No."

He brushed his lips against her neck before meeting her gaze.

"I want you, Hazel. But I can see the hesitation in your eyes." He leaned closer to her, never breaking her gaze. "Let go of your reservations. Let me make love to you. Let me give you something you've never had."

"I've had sex before, John."

"But you've never made love with a man who would go to so much trouble just to have you." He grinned slyly. "No more resistance. Let me have you, Hazel."

She couldn't think. Desire was in his eyes. Need was filling her. Four years of need, to be precise. "I don't want to feed any illusions, John. I'm not her. I'm not—"

"This isn't about Alison. This is about you. And me." He wrapped an arm around her waist and drew her closer. "And this." He kissed her. There was no sensual or seductive undertone to it. It was pure and raw lust. He seized her mouth, thrusting his tongue against her own.

He withdrew and picked her up off the bed. He set her down on top of the dresser that rested against the wall. His mouth was instantly on her neck, but this was no light pressure from his lips like she had experienced before. This was his most primal hunger unleashing. He sucked and nibbled along her neck as his hands worked to loosen the bun in her hair. For her own part, she clutched his shoulders with her hands, unsure if she should stop this madness or just surrender.

She wanted to stop him. She was so afraid that he was picturing Alison in her place—despite his assurance that he wasn't. She did not want to play the part of the surrogate in this act of passion. She wanted him to want her, *Hazel*. Hazel the mother, Hazel the lost coward, and Hazel the writer—who put everything in her soul on discounted notepad because revealing to the world what spilled out was too terrifying. She wanted him to want *that* Hazel. Not Alison.

But she wanted so badly to just surrender—no matter his real intentions—and to let John have everything he wanted.

His hands succeeded in freeing her hair from the half-dozen bobby pins. He pushed her legs apart and stepped between them. The look in his eyes frightened her—she had never seen a man so determined.

"Kiss me," he gasped, "Kiss me, Hazel."

She obeyed and set her lips against his. He took control again, thrusting his tongue inside her mouth in a raw preview of what he was working toward. She broke the kiss, gasping for breath, panting shamefully.

In the arms of her abductor—she would surely be the new poster girl for Stockholm syndrome.

His kiss continued down to her throat, and his hands gripped her back, slowly moving to her hips. He not so shyly breached her breasts. She moaned as his hands caressed her until her nipples had hardened through both her bra and her dress.

He stopped caressing her into madness and rested his hands on her hips. Ruthlessly, he rubbed the erection that was tenting his trousers against her panties. She was losing the will to stop him.

She arched her back as he tipped his head to kiss her breasts. Her nipples, still hard, he suckled through the material of her clothing…and it was quickly becoming not enough.

He began feverishly unbuttoning the top of her dress. As each button snapped open, they were both fully aware that they were about to make a critical decision.

The last button rested at her waist. He unsnapped it and ran his hands from her belly up to her breasts and neck. She moaned louder. He grabbed the open shoulders of the dress and yanked it down her arms. Kissing her neck, he reached around and unhooked her bra. He discarded it immediately and cupped her naked breasts before seizing one taut nipple in his mouth.

Hazel cried out and wrapped her legs around his hips; her arms went around his neck, and her hands pulled the short strands of his hair.

"So beautiful," he murmured. "Feel me, Hazel. Feel me."

She couldn't stop feeling him. His hands caressed her bare back as his mouth continued to suckle and kiss her breasts.

"Feel me, Hazel," he pulled one of her hands to his trousers and rubbed it against his erection. "Feel me."

She understood and unzipped what he had been holding back. He withdrew his mouth from her breast and impatiently pulled his cock out of his boxers. The erection was even more impressive than she had envisioned. It was large and demanding—much like John's himself. And when he pushed it between her legs and began rubbing himself against the slick satin of her panties, she thought she would die.

One hand gripped her hip while the other caressed her breast again. All the while, that friction was creating a monstrous wave of desire. She needed—wanted—all of him. Immediately. But the way he stroked her, she was going to come. She was going to come very quickly. Too quickly.

"Let go, my darling. Let go and surrender." He reached down to pull the rest of her dress off—and her panties along with it. "Let go, my love. Come to me. Come to me!"

The words he spoke—the words of the stranger in her dream— made her panic. Then the memory of that awful woman standing at the foot of her bed returned. And in that instant, she knew she had to retreat.

But before she could push John away, he thrust a finger inside of her and lightly pinched her clit. She grabbed his shoulders, coming with an intensity she had never experienced.

"John!" She nearly shrieked his name. "Please, stop!"

He looked at her confused. "I don't think I can." He panted.

"John, please!" She clutched her dress before he had it off her hips. Her panties hung halfway down her thighs. "Please stop!"

He withdrew from between her legs, his cock still swollen and thick with need. "Hazel, what's wrong?"

She pushed herself off the dresser and pulled her dress back over her breasts. She was shaking her head wildly at him. "I'm sorry—I can't do this."

He looked stricken as he tried to fasten his trousers back over his bulging cock. "I don't understand. What did I do?"

The words he had spoken—they were still echoing in her head. "Why did you say that?"

His face was a mixture of worry and confusion. And pain—probably from his lower region. "Why did I ask what I did?"

"No! Why did you—why did you tell me to come to you?"

He shook his head. "Hazel, I want you. I still want you. Very, *very* badly."

She shook her head erratically again. "But it was your wording! Your wording was just like his!"

"His?"

"Yes!"

"Duncan?"

"No—the man! The man who was in my dream! He spoke those words right before I woke up and saw that woman in my room!"

He stepped toward her, clearly expecting her to run. Instead, she stood frozen. Frightened. "Hazel," he cupped her face. "I don't know what to say."

"Are you playing some kind of game with me, John?" Her voice stammered. "Is this some sick and twisted way to get me into bed with you?"

"What? You aren't making any sense!"

"To scare me into your arms—to make me think you are the only one I can turn to!"

"Is that what you think?" He looked devastated. "Hazel, there was no woman—or man. I was outside nearly all night searching, remember? There is no stranger."

She couldn't think. It was too much to process.

"Hazel, please stay here. We need to talk about this. But first I have to…" He walked toward the bathroom, already unzipping his strained trousers.

He shut the bathroom door behind him. Hazel slumped onto the bed, unsure of what had just happened.

She had almost made love with St. Jerome's most eligible bachelor, John Stonem—the man who had abducted her and her daughter. The man who was promising her a new start. The man who may be hiding more secrets than she could fathom.

Chapter Eighteen

Scotty did most of the talking through breakfast. It seemed to John that Hazel was going overboard trying to be friendly and cordial to Laura, who was eyeing both her and Scotty with great suspicion. But Hazel would not face John.

John, on the other hand, couldn't take his eyes off her. They had nearly made love last night—until he had said the wrong thing.

Except it had never been the wrong thing. It had been what he always uttered to Alison. And in the throes of passion, Alison would, indeed, come for him.

And sure, maybe John should come up with some new material, but it had been a long time since he had felt an emotional connection with a woman—twenty *years* to be exact—and saying those words to Hazel felt completely natural.

It rattled him to the core that this woman, Hazel, was responding so wildly to words that only Alison would remember. Hazel would have no way of knowing that those words—and the tone in which he spoke them—were something he had only ever said to Alison. Unless she *was* remembering a former life. Unless their night together and those words he had spoken had triggered more than just a bad dream.

What if he sparked a lost memory?

Yet she felt so different from Alison when he touched her. Hazel was so sensual that it undid him. Her kiss, so thorough and deep. There was an unmistakable desire inside of her that he sensed she wanted to unleash, but her unwavering caution kept that part of her subdued. She was so guarded. He wanted to free her.

Alison, by contrast, had always been wild and carefree in bed. There was no caution or hesitation.

But Hazel Loveless, so full of secrets and restrained passion.

He felt alive in Hazel's arms—and he would do anything to have her. She haunted his dreams; he wanted her *now*.

And it was irritating the shit out of him that she wouldn't make eye contact with him—or even look in his direction.

Instead, all her attention was on Scotty and Laura.

John had wanted so badly to talk about what had happened last night, but when he emerged from the bathroom, there was a note on the dresser from Hazel stating she was sleeping in Scotty's room for the night. It was one hell of an aggravation, but out of respect, he left her alone. He figured morning would be the next best opportunity, except he forgot about Laura's presence, and he forgot how chatty a four-year-old could be.

"Mommy and I like picking dandelions."

John could see the boredom in Laura's face, but she carried on with the conversation anyway. "Dandelions?"

"Yeah! Pretty, yellowy flowers! We pick them all the time when it's nice outside."

"You know, dandelions are not really flowers. They're weeds, dear. Nasty, garden-ruining weeds. I pay my gardener Carlos a bonus just for killing them all." Laura winked at the girl. "*Muerto* to all of them!"

"Huh?" Scotty made a horrified face and turned her head to the side as if Laura had just told her Santa Claus was dead.

"They're not to everyone's taste," John chimed in. "But I think they are absolutely beautiful." He shot Laura a warning look, and then cast a big smile on Scotty.

"I would *never* kill a dandelion. Even if it *is* just a weed!" The little girl's eyes were wide with disbelief.

"Some things are just not worth keeping alive, dear."

He sighed heavily at her remark, and was genuinely thrilled when Laura left the room.

"Mommy," Scotty whispered, "Mrs. Winkles and me don't like that mean lady." She held the doll up and made it shake its head up and down.

"Scotty, that isn't nice!"

"Mommy, I'm about to spaz out!"

"'Spaz out'? Scotty, where did you learn that?"

"*Inside Edition*. Me and Benny have a TV schedule." Both John and Hazel glanced at Bennings, who was clearing away Laura's plate.

John saw the old man shrug, but wasn't sure if the old man saw both his and Hazel's disapproving stares.

"A man can only watch so much *Sesame Street* until the real world summons him back."

"*Inside Edition* is the real world, Bennings?" John's eyebrow was cocked sternly.

"*The Real World* is on MTV," Scotty added quickly. "We watch reruns in the afternoons!"

John thought Hazel's eyes were about to pop out of their sockets. "Ahem, come now, Scotty. We have dishes to do."

Scotty plopped off her chair and giddily followed Bennings with Mrs. Winkles in tow.

Now only John and Hazel remained at the table.

"Not that I thought I was going to be nominated for mother of the year, but wow. Big mom-fail."

"I'll have a talk with Bennings. She shouldn't be watching that garbage."

"I'm not spending enough time with her."

John balked. "You're with that girl sixteen hours a day. She spends an hour in the morning and an hour in the afternoon with Bennings. The rest of the time you're both sleeping."

Hazel stood up and picked up her plate. "You're right."

"Except for last night."

+++

Hazel froze and finally looked at him. She didn't want to talk about last night, but she could tell by his expression that she was not getting out of it.

"I don't regret last night, Hazel. I only regret that we didn't finish what we started."

"I couldn't finish."

"But you came, Hazel. Didn't you?"

She faced him fully and glared. "My daughter is just in the other room!"

She knew he too was angry. She saw his hands as they gripped his side of the table. "What you stopped last night wasn't the end. Sooner or later, we'll finish what we started."

"No. We won't finish anything, John. I can't go back to that moment."

"Can't or won't?"

"Both!"

"So you regret what we did last night?" He stepped around the table and put his arms around her waist. She tried to push away, but he held her firmly. "You regret kissing me?" He pulled her closer.

"You regret this?" He drew his hand around to her abdomen and started moving it up.

"John," her voice was breathless again. She was ashamed to be so aroused by this man—her kidnapper.

"You regret this?" He cupped her breast, kneading her nipple until she whimpered. "I thought not." He brushed his lips against hers. "Let's go upstairs and finish what we started."

Sanity was somehow restored. "No," she gently pushed his roaming hands away. "I can't."

She started walking away from him.

"They were just words, Hazel. It doesn't change what's between us."

"They were words that a stranger whispered to me."

"In a dream, Hazel!" John took a deep breath. "Maybe last night just moved too fast for you." He was offering her an escape. And an opportunity for a redo, if she wanted it. She couldn't take it.

"Maybe I don't know that I can trust you."

Her dagger hit its mark. "Maybe you just wanted an excuse. Seduce the pathetic widower. And withdraw because you're too fucking scared to take a risk."

"What?"

"You are so blinded by let-downs that I don't know if you are even capable of feeling love."

"That is bullshit! I love my daughter more than anything—but I certainly wouldn't kidnap her to make her love me in return!" Another ugly truth. She regretted the words, but she wouldn't take them back.

"The love you feel for your daughter is different. She's dependent on you—not the other way around. You're used to being all on your own. You're not brave enough to have it any other way. And *that* is why you will always reject love. It could march right up to you and slap you in the face and you still wouldn't have it. Because feeling it and returning it to a man would mean you'd have to depend on him and lean on him—and that frightens you! You'd rather be on your single-mother high horse than follow your heart!"

Raw fury made her voice guttural. "You could *never* understand! You aren't a parent! I have to show her the right way so she doesn't make the same mistakes I made! I have to show her that she can grow up and be a capable woman, a strong woman. A woman who doesn't need help from anyone!"

"Does help not include a quarter of a million dollars?"

"Oh, goddamn you!" Tears fell from her eyes.

"No, goddamn you!" He grabbed her hips and shoved her against the counter. "Goddamn you for wearing *her* face and making me have hope that she had returned to me. But you aren't her! You could never be her! And I was ready to accept that and love you anyway—love you for yourself!"

She struggled in his arms. "Love me for myself? As some lousy second place in your larger-than-life game of love! That's a really great reward! I may not be able to recite poems or even halfway mimic what you and your *dead wife* had, but I know that no woman wants to be settled for."

He raised his hand as if to slap her, but caught himself and slammed his fist into the counter instead.

"Yes, hit me, John. Show me how great your love is! Tell me how much like Alison I am—her fucking doppelganger!"

"I never struck Alison. Never came close. But you—" He stepped quickly away from her.

He fled up the stairs, leaving Hazel to her own dreadful tears.

+++

She walked the garden path, unsure what she should do. All the terrible things she had said to John.

She couldn't help it. He had hurt her so badly. She *was* capable of feeling love for a man—but Scotty had to come first. That's just the way it was.

She did feel something for John, as much as she fought against it. In the beginning, she was repulsed by John's actions. Then she felt the attraction between them—worse, she fed into it. And now...now she genuinely felt she had feelings for him. But she wasn't so sure about John. After the fight they just had, she was certain he only thought of her *at best* as a second-rate Alison. Not as Hazel Loveless.

An old, bitter wound felt raw again. Hazel was once again a disappointment. She couldn't be a proper substitute for that lost sunshine child...or even a dead woman.

"Well, hello."

She wasn't expecting company, and she tried to cover up her tears before facing John's sister.

"Laura, I didn't notice you there."

John's sister was standing under a trellis, looking as though she had stepped out of an Anne Klein ad. Hazel was forced to wear Alison's clothes day after day—and while they were all stunning dresses and suits, they were supremely outdated. Laura's clothes were at the height of current fashion. They might even be the same clothes Alison herself would wear if she were still alive.

"I've been watching you for a while now."

"Oh." She wiped away the rest of her tears. "I'm just having a rough morning."

"It's okay, dear. I know why you're upset. The real reason you're upset, I mean."

Hazel stared at her, puzzled.

"I know what John did."

She turned bright red. How loud had they been last night?

"I know that he orchestrated your stay here."

Relief—and embarrassment—trickled through her body. "Laura, I—"

"You don't have to say anything, Hazel. Really, you don't. I know my brother. And I knew he had done something terrible the moment I laid eyes on you."

Hazel rubbed her face. It felt grainy and dirty from all the crying she had done. "John has the best intentions, I'm sure of that."

"Oh, yes. He always does, dear. He truly always does. But he's sick, you see."

"He's in perpetual mourning."

Laura reached out and took Hazel's hands in her own. "It's more than that. He's delusional about his relationship with Alison in the first place. You see, when she died, well, he somehow romanticized their marriage. But it wasn't all flowers and sunshine. Believe me. I lived with John and Alison at the time."

Hazel was stunned. This was the first indication she'd heard that John and Alison's marriage wasn't a larger-than-life love story. "It's true, though John may never come to terms with that truth. He had an affair while they were married."

"What?" Hazel felt like the wind had been knocked out of her.

"It's true. I know for a fact. And that's why, dear Hazel, you don't have to tell me a thing. I already know what he's done."

She was baffled. "John had an affair while he was married to Alison? I can't believe it."

Hazel quelled the instinctual revulsion she felt when Laura patted her forearm. "Well, not everything is as glorious as yellowy dandelions. And that's why, for all of our safety, I'm going to start the legal paperwork to get John committed."

Hazel's jaw dropped. "Committed?"

"Yes. I see no other way."

"Laura, you can't just lock him up!"

"Actually, with your signature on this affidavit, I can do exactly that." She pulled a folder off the bench near the trellis. "This is part of a statement showing John's severe mental health issues. It includes a very brief synopsis of his actions in regards to you and your daughter. I highlighted specific sections in yellow for your review." She smiled widely, and then added, "I would be sure to read over the specifics, if I were you."

Hazel was chilled by Laura's news. Not just about the committal papers—but also by her statement that John had been unfaithful to Alison. Was that why John remained so loyal to Alison's memory? Out of guilt?

But there had to be more to it than that. She didn't really trust Laura to reveal all the pertinent facts. There was something about the woman that made Hazel uneasy. She just couldn't put her finger on what.

Chapter Nineteen

Hazel paced her bedroom in a panic. She had to grab Scotty and get the hell out of the house. With every passing second, her panic grew.

She felt like a fool—all those moments with John where she genuinely felt something, and he had almost gotten Scotty killed.

The paperwork Laura gave her lay spread out on her bed, and there, highlighted in yellow: *"So he cut the brakes..."*

Hazel was beyond disgusted. She had touched this monster.

In the wardrobe, Hazel pulled out one of Alison Stonem's winter coats. If Laura had rented a boat, then that would be Hazel's way out. She'd grab Scotty and make a run for it.

She could feel the tears burning her eyes. How could John have done this? How could he?

But she knew that awful answer, and she had to leave. As she put on some borrowed boots, another revelation hit her: John wasn't the only person in the world to lose his spouse. Plenty of other widowers managed to move on with their lives without kidnapping innocent women. Laura must be right—he must be crazy. Crazy with grief, and with guilt over his affair.

What John had done was inexcusable.

Hazel stormed into Scotty's bedroom. The child was napping, and the sound of Scotty's contented snores echoed throughout the room.

Scotty had trusted John.

Rage boiled inside of Hazel.

She couldn't just grab Scotty and leave—not yet. She still had questions. A volume of questions. Laura Stonem had set a bomb off by not only giving Hazel John's head on a silver platter, but by exposing his troubled marriage.

Still, could Laura be trusted? In less than two days, she had completely disrupted Hazel's life. If John's sister was just money-hungry, maybe she was making up these accusations. Yet the lengths that John had gone to in kidnapping her and Scotty made Hazel believe John could very well have cut the brakes, if he thought it was necessary. John's actions in the short time she knew him only proved he was capable of that and more.

She couldn't wait any longer. She needed real answers, not the half-truths she was getting from John.

She hid the coat and boats, crept out of Scotty's bedroom, and wandered down to the kitchen. To her relief, Bennings was there alone.

"Do you have a minute?"

The old man turned and gave her a friendly smile. "Of course, Miss Hazel."

"Well, first of all, where are John and Laura?"

"Miss Laura is in the garden. I'm not sure where Mr. John is presently."

"Bennings"—she was trying not to sound panicked—"Laura showed me an affidavit this morning. She wants to commit John."

She watched the poor man's eyes nearly bulge out of his head.

"She knows what John did to get me and Scotty here." She saw the man flinch. "And yes, Bennings, I know what he did, too."

"Miss Hazel, I must confess something. Mr. John…well, you see…"

She waved her hand up at him. "Bennings, I get it. You want to protect John. But I want the truth now."

He sat down at the table and offered her coffee. She took a seat across from the old man and stared him down. "Is it true, Bennings? Did he cut the brakes?"

She watched as Bennings stared guiltily into his coffee. He looked horribly conflicted, but finally responded. "Mr. John is capable of many acts. Great love being both his best trait and worst fault."

"And that great love equated to kidnapping, didn't it?"

"Mr. John is a wonderful provider—and a protector, when needed."

She laughed dryly at his words, but the man seemed ominously serious. "This hardly makes what Laura is trying to do seem bad, does it?"

"Miss Hazel, I have never betrayed Mr. John's trust. But I will now. As his actions were to protect me, I must now protect him."

"To protect *you*? What are you talking about?"

"Miss Hazel, it was not Mr. John who orchestrated your kidnapping. I did it."

She was certain she misunderstood him. "What?"

"John had no part in your attendance at the gala. I arranged everything."

She suddenly pitied Bennings. He was ready to take the fall for John's actions. "Bennings, I think it's touching how loyal you are to John, but you're doing him no favors in covering for him. Don't you see that?"

"Miss Hazel, I arranged your invitation to the gala. I wanted Mr. John to see you. I wanted him to see in you what I saw when I first noticed you at the grocery store."

She was going to be sick. "The grocery store?"

"Yes. I saw you there on a Saturday. I was nearly spellbound because I couldn't believe the face I was seeing. It was as if the past had finally caught up with the present. I saw hope for Mr. John."

"Bennings…" She was grateful she was sitting down.

"I will confess I manipulated the brakes on the taxi that was to take you home. But I didn't think it would cause great harm. You see, I was driving it. I merely meant to cause the slightest accident, Miss Hazel. I never intended injury. It's just that I didn't feel right letting you go. Not when you and Mr. John didn't even speak at the gala—"

"So you risked my life and my daughter's to perpetuate a fantasy? Is that what you're saying? Oh my God, Bennings!"

"A thousand apologies wouldn't be enough, Miss Hazel. I never wished to cause any harm or injury—not to you and especially not to little Scotty."

She wanted to cry. If he was telling the truth, John was at least in part innocent. But it also created a whole new slew of questions. "Why did John say he did it if it was you all along?"

"I made a mistake in the past, Miss Hazel."

"Are you saying I'm not your first kidnapping?"

"No, Miss—nothing like that! I had a drinking problem years ago. There was an accident and a woman was injured. I regret telling you that it was not my first violation, but it was the most severe and the very last time it happened. I believe Mr. John is trying to protect me by offering to pay you."

So…John was innocent of her kidnapping, and the money he was giving her wasn't a ploy to keep her in the house for a month. It was to protect his butler.

She had completed misread the situation, and she wondered why that upset her. During the odd but brief time with John, she was falling hard for him. She had hoped maybe he might fall for her too. The real her—not the Alison look-a-like. But Bennings's revelation proved just how foolish that wish was.

"You're lucky John cares so much for you, Bennings," she remarked bitterly. "But I barely know you. So tell me: Why shouldn't I call the police? You caused this!"

"I know, Miss Hazel. I'm so sorry. I'd undo this if I could, I swear to you."

She shook her head. "I won't call the police, but only because I don't see how it would serve John if his only friend were put behind bars."

He looked relieved. Or saddened. She wasn't entirely sure.

"I'm afraid for Mr. John. If he doesn't confess to Miss Laura about what I've done…"

"That does put you in a precarious situation, doesn't it? Is it all for the money, do you think, or does Laura have some kind of grudge against John?"

"Miss Laura has always had her own agenda, and I fear for Mr. John when she's here. I fear for all of us."

A chill went up her spine. There was something frightening about his tone. "Why, Bennings? What did she do?"

"I can't speak without proof, Miss Hazel. But I've long suspected—"

The back door sprung open. An exasperated sigh echoed through the main floor.

"Bennings? Is there any coffee? I'm half-frozen!"

"In the kitchen, Miss Laura."

Hazel noted the look of warning from Bennings.

"Oh, Hazel Loveless." Laura's breezy, sing-songy way of speaking was becoming faker by the minute. "I'm hoping you have a signed copy of that contract I gave you earlier."

"I don't have it on me, Laura."

She brushed what must have been imaginary debris off her pants. "Oh, then later you can give it to me, yes?" Her smile made Hazel uncomfortable. She was dying to talk to John. She needed the truth from him—she needed to know everything.

"Has Bennings been filling your ears with family stories?" She giggled maniacally. "Good old Bennings. He's been a trusted family friend forever. And loyal—fiercely loyal. He is truly one of a kind."

Hazel nodded. Loyal enough to commit a felony!

"Bennings, would you mind leaving us two ladies alone for a bit? I'm hoping Hazel will come on a little shopping excursion with me later."

Silently, Bennings left the kitchen. Hazel took the opportunity to dig for more information.

"Laura, when we were talking earlier, you mentioned John had been unfaithful to Alison."

"I did." She sipped her coffee. "And he was."

"Did Alison know?"

Hazel was fixated on Laura, who looked like she didn't have a care in the world as she stirred more creamer into her coffee. "I suppose she did."

"Well, I guess I want to ask how *you* know about the affair."

Hazel watched Laura closely as she readjusted in her seat. "Oh, that's a valid question, I suppose. One night John drunk himself into a stupor—which he often did back then—and he confessed to me."

"He just told you he slept with another woman? He told his own sister?"

Judging by the scowl on Laura's face, Hazel knew she'd hit a nerve. "John and I are the only Stonems left. We're essentially one and the same. We keep no secrets."

"I'm sorry—I didn't mean to offend you. I'm an only child, so I guess I don't understand the sibling bond."

"I should say you don't, or you wouldn't ask such a stupid question." The harshness in her voice caught Hazel off guard. But Laura immediately withdrew. "Dearest Hazel." The fake tone had returned. "Let's be friends, okay? You've been caught in a terrible scheme by my brother, and I want to do whatever possible to help you and your darling little child get out of here so you can pick up the pieces of your darling little lives."

"I'm just asking for the truth, Laura. I'm not trying to be unfriendly."

"Of course you aren't being unfriendly!"

Hazel was growing more and more uncomfortable being alone with Laura. And Bennings's earlier warning wasn't helping matters. "I'm going to check on Scotty. We can pick this up later, right?"

"We will, Hazel. And don't worry—whatever we agree upon, John needn't know about."

"I thought you said there were no secrets between you two?"

Hazel cringed when Laura winked at her. "Well, this is for John's own good."

+++

John sat silently in Hazel's bedroom. He had intended to apologize for his behavior. He had intended to tell her that he loved her—and that it didn't matter if she wasn't Alison. Hell, he himself had begun to believe that his initial assumption was correct, that it was nothing more than a coincidence. She was merely a woman who looked like his late wife. Nothing more.

In the time Hazel had been in his house, John felt himself changing. Hazel wasn't really like Alison. Alison had seen the world in vibrant colors. She seized opportunities by throwing herself at them. Hazel approached life with gentleness and caution. She guarded herself and her feelings.

Alison had a lousy childhood with her alcoholic father. When she was free of that tie, she pounced on life. She took risks. She hung out of windows in her leisure time. Hazel had no memory of her early years. She lived in the shadow of her former self with a mother who would do anything to trade the new Hazel for the old one. What hell that must have been.

He even thought he understood why Hazel had chosen a guy like Duncan—he was just as emotionally unavailable as she was.

John sat in her chair and dropped his sister's affidavit to the floor in disgust. In his hand, he held Hazel's notepad. Pages and pages were filled out with her own words—not the carefully crafted responses she always gave to outsiders. No, these words, they were her private thoughts. They were her real fears. He read every word. *Every* word. And he found himself transfixed and enthralled with her all the more.

He walked with no purpose from one side of the room to another.

Every woman in sight had her eyes on him. I had my eyes on him.

I wished just once he would turn my way.

He remembered that night so well. He remembered the green dress that clung to her body. But her face and her eyes—he couldn't risk looking her way. He couldn't risk another round of hurt. And disappointment.

Will my baby remember these strange days? Did I ever live strange days before

the accident? The mirror of my image changed. The eyes of that sunshine child so

round and bright. The eyes of just Hazel so almond-like. Half open and half shut,

but I see his world. I want his world.

In every page he read her constant struggle. To stay hidden and aloof, or to come out from the shadows and let the world in. He wanted to hold her. He wanted to tell her that she shouldn't be afraid.

What has happened to me? He looks at me like he knows every inch of me, body and soul, but I'm not her. I'm not her. I'm not her. It's Beth again. Beth, when I wouldn't put my ballet shoes on. Beth, when I didn't go to college. It's John. John, when I couldn't meet his eyes. John, when I couldn't bear to look at her picture. John, when I saw the woman in my room. The woman in my room!

I don't want to need John. I don't want to love John. I just want to touch him, just once.

Maybe he needs me.

That last sentence—he read it and felt his own tear wet his hand. "Of course I need you, my darling," he whispered to himself.

"John, what are you doing?"

He wasn't expecting to see Hazel standing in the doorway gawking at him. And he sure as hell wasn't expecting her to find him guiltily holding her notepad. One thing was for sure, though. The woman he loved had murder in her eyes.

+++

"John, I just asked you a question." She was trying her damnedest to stay calm, but reading her notepad was beyond crossing the line. He seemed cavalier about it, which did nothing but anger her more.

"I saw the affidavit on your bed. Are you teaming up with Laura?"

She wanted to punch him, and oddly, she felt he wanted that reaction from her. "Did you go through my things? Did you read what's in that notepad?"

"Hazel, I just want to know if you're my ally or Laura's. I need to know whom I can trust." His face was blank, while she knew hers showed clear agitation. "I know you've been talking to Laura."

"Your sister seems to think you are unbalanced."

"She's not the most trustworthy person."

She glared at John. "That seems to run in the family."

He stood up from her chair—the chair she had been resting in right before they almost made love. "So you know everything now. You know every disgusting step I took in abducting you and your child."

"Yes, John. You cut the brake line. The car almost went over the bridge, and my child could have been killed. All because I look like your dead wife." She expected him to flinch. Instead, he faced her with the most agonized expression she had ever seen. "Except I know it wasn't you."

That *did* make him flinch. "The statement I gave Laura is in that affidavit."

"Give it up, John. Your butler confessed that this was his idea, not yours. And the money you're paying me in exchange for staying here is to save him."

"I know you aren't Alison. And saying sorry a thousand times won't matter. I won't mean it anyway."

"'Cause you didn't do it!" she snapped. "It was the butler with the candlestick in the library. And you would do anything to save him." She stepped away from him.

"Hazel, I'm in love with you."

"Quite a departure considering you wanted to hit me downstairs."

"I would never hit you."

She shook her head. It was impossible for John to feel love for anyone but Alison. "You're in love with the past, John. Not me. You're in love with the idea that you could have a piece of Alison back. But it's not me. You don't even know me."

"I don't know you?" He reached out and lightly stroked her cheek. She should stop him. She should tell him to leave. Instead, she let him continue. "The woman who has worked like hell to stay independent and alone in an unfair world? The woman who has sacrificed everything—herself, her own happiness—just to make sure her child has better? The woman who is so afraid to disappoint the people she loves that she guards her thoughts in a vault?"

Tears streaked her face, but she couldn't surrender to his words. Not now.

"I know you, Hazel. I know you well. I see that you aren't Alison, and I can accept that. You are the only human being on this earth who can make me feel like life is worth living again. Do you know what a feat that is? To make me want to live again after two decades of despair? You suppress an emptiness, Hazel, that I thought would claim me one day, and even though Bennings was the mastermind behind your kidnapping, I'd do anything to keep you here now." He wrapped his arms around her waist. Again, she should push him away. But she couldn't. "And so I have to ask you—are you going to sign that affidavit?"

Chapter Twenty

"You know I won't sign it." Her answer nearly brought him to his knees. "But I want to talk to you about Laura. Because she told me your marriage to Alison wasn't quite so legendary."

"What?" He could tell she was building up to something, and whatever it was, it was making him uneasy. "What has Laura said about my marriage?"

"She said you cheated on Alison."

Her words were like daggers. "Hazel, I *never* cheated on Alison! That doesn't even make sense! Why would Laura say that?"

"She said you were drunk."

"Drunk?" He paced toward the door. "I never cheated on Alison. I never even entertained the idea then."

"What do you mean by 'then'?"

He turned around to face her. "I meant what I said, Hazel. I'm in love with you. But I understand if you don't feel the same way."

"I don't know what I feel, John. No one has invaded my privacy the way you have." She was talking about the notepad. He knew it was wrong, but her writings had given him insight into her soul—and he felt he knew this woman now. He finally felt he could let Alison go.

"I'm sorry, Hazel. It won't happen again." He saw doubt in her eyes, but he wasn't a fool. It would take time to gain her trust.

"It better not, John. It's bad enough that your creepy sister is snooping around."

He stole a kiss in that moment. A long, lingering kiss. "Let me handle this business with Laura. When she tried to go behind my back to commit me before, the ulterior motive was money. This time she seems to be trying to use you."

"I hate to say this, but with everything you've taken responsibility for, it wouldn't be hard to get you committed. Or even sent to prison."

"For everything I've done to you and Scotty, I deserve it. But I can't fail Bennings. He's been with me to hell and back." He cupped her face in his hands. "I expected you to grab Scotty and flee to the police if you found out. Aren't you angry? Furious?"

"I am."

"Do you want to take your revenge out on me?" He knew he was goading her into a repeat of the other night, but he couldn't help it. "Come on, hit me."

He knew the rage inside of her was still brewing, but he wasn't expecting a swift left-handed punch to hit gut. He wheezed, and he saw a supreme look of satisfaction in her eyes. Despite the pain, he was happy to see her react so unreservedly.

He put his arm out as if to get a reprieve from another blow. "Feel better?" he asked breathlessly.

"I could probably punch you all night. I should have done at least that to Duncan all those years ago."

"I'd like to land a few blows on Duncan. But first, I need to deal with Laura."

"John, I have a bad feeling about her."

"Do me a favor and stay put. I'll have her out of this house tonight."

John left Hazel alone. He was hopeful she would reflect on their talk. He was hopeful she would accept his apology and even forgive him—and Bennings. But there was still Laura to deal with.

It wasn't very hard to find her. John guessed she would be rummaging through Alison's bedroom, and no surprise, that's exactly where she was. The affidavit was more than enough to enlist his rage. But finding her treasure hunting in his late wife's room was bringing him closer to the edge.

"Can I help you with something, my sweet and innocent sister?"

She spun around abruptly to face him. "I was waiting for you and what's-her-face's heart-to-heart to end. Very touching, by the way."

"Spying at your age? That's a new low."

"Oh, yes. Tell me about new lows, John. I just heard you confess your love to a woman you kidnapped—excuse me—a woman that old man kidnapped. A woman who just so happens to be a dead-ringer for your dead wife!"

"Get out of this house and take this goddamn thing with you!" He flung the affidavit at her.

"You're kicking me out? Again? John, I'm trying to save you!"

"No, you're a spoiled bitch who's just after the money! It's always come down to the money. James tried to warn me, and I just couldn't get on board. I couldn't believe that my poor, mistreated sister was a lost cause. James was seldom right about anything, but sadly, I think he had you pegged from the start." He spotted the tears in her eyes, and he rolled his eyes.

"Is that what you really think, John? 'Cause it's not true! I care about you! I love you! James was evil. He and mother never loved me. But you, you always said you'd take care of me. I'm just trying to take care of *you* now—"

"Enough!" He was out of patience. Laura had betrayed him again. And he had welcomed her back, even thought he could trust her. "I was willing to give you another chance and this is how you repay me. Get out!"

"You'll be sorry, John. I was coming home this time. I was coming home to take care of you!"

"You were coming to take care of yourself, Laura. I've had enough. For the first time in a long time, I found someone to share my life with. I don't need your deceptions!" He was beyond anger. Beyond rage. He grabbed her by the shoulders. "Why did you tell Hazel I cheated on Alison? That never happened!"

"It did! Don't you remember, John? Don't you remember that night?"

He shoved her against the wall, the force more than he had intended, but the anger was billowing out of control. She winced and struggled against him.

"This is my life, whatever I have left of it!"

"I came here out of love, John! I love you! I love you!" Each time she said it, he shoved her harder against the wall.

"John, stop!" The sound of Hazel's voice froze him. He could have killed Laura. He could have slammed her head into the wall as many times as it took. Instead, he withdrew.

"You hurt me! She saw you!" Laura screamed.

"Scotty heard you screaming. I had to send her downstairs with Bennings."

"I'm sorry, Hazel." John's gaze fell onto Hazel, and for a moment, they locked eyes. It was a moment of desperation. And it was one Laura might expose.

"Attempted murder. I don't need her goddamn signature to get you committed!"

"Laura, please," Hazel pleaded. "Just go. Please."

John felt Hazel's hand gripping his forearm—and saw the look of contempt on his own sister's face at the gentle gesture.

"Don't come back here for money or fake notions of love. Don't come back here at all." John's voice was raw, but Hazel's hands were anchoring him to the floor.

"You'd deny me when you've taken everything from me, John? You'll be sorry for this!" Her words confused him. What had he ever taken from her?

Before he could ask, Laura fled the room.

John looked down at Hazel's hands still clutching his forearm.

"I'll apologize for scaring Scotty."

"God, what happened, John? Why did you attack her like that?"

He pulled her into his arms—instantly relieved that she didn't push him away.

It was Hazel he was holding. Hazel he was lusting after. Hazel he was in love with.

He became more certain in that moment that Alison was gone. Hazel's guarded cautiousness and unwavering need to protect those she cared about were not traits of Alison's.

Also, Alison was carefree, but she didn't like to be left alone for too long. Hazel had been alone her entire life. The more John looked into Hazel's eyes, the more the truth was etched into his brain. Hazel was Hazel. Alison was gone.

And in one strained breath, John was finally letting go of the chokehold he had on Alison's presence.

"John." Hazel's voice warmed his heart. But he instantly remembered his sister's latest betrayal.

"Laura was spying on us. Mocking me. Telling me that I'm only in love with you because of who you look like." He paused to read her face. "Do you think that as well?"

+++

"I don't know what to think, John."

"It's you I love, Hazel. It's all you. Not a memory."

Hazel wanted to concentrate on John's words, but a strange sensation suddenly overcame her.

Her attention was immediately drawn to the door. Goose bumps ran over her body like a tidal wave. There was something urgent she had to do. There was something in the hallway that was beckoning her presence.

"Hazel? What is it?" John's voice was a mere echo compared to the darkness that was filling her mind. Not darkness—but the looming of that awful black water.

"Something's wrong." She left John's arms and peered down the hallway.

Her stomach was in a knot. A blast of chilled air swept past her, and for a moment, every cell in her body felt frozen. No, not frozen: wet. She felt cold and wet. And while she worked to overcome the sensation, her eyes adjusted to another horror.

At the top of the stairs was the woman—that ghoulish woman Hazel had prayed was a hallucination.

Her back was to Hazel again. The stringy hair was plastered against her gown. And for a moment, Hazel was sure the woman murmured a single word: "*Hurry.*" The woman raised her arm straight out to her side and dangled something out of her hand. That doll…Scotty's doll. The woman began to fade away, but before the last figment of her ghastly appearance was gone, she dropped Mrs. Winkles down the stairs, the same stairs Scotty had descended with Bennings. The very stairs Laura had likely descended.

"Scotty!" Hazel raced down them with John right behind her.

"What is it? What did you see?"

She didn't respond but ran faster—harder—desperate to get to Scotty, and having an ominous fear that it was already too late.

"Hazel, what's happening? Tell me!"

Instead, she started screaming for Scotty. And then they both stopped abruptly. There was a thin trail of blood leading to the kitchen. "God, no!"

John pushed her behind him and walked cautiously to the kitchen. There were no sounds coming from within. He reached around the wall to flip the lights on.

"No!" Hazel's voice screeched behind him. The kitchen table was broken, and lying underneath the rubble was Bennings.

John quickly pulled the pieces of wood off the old man. "Is he okay?"

John felt for a pulse, and when he found one, he carefully he pulled the man out from the rest of the debris. "Bennings, can you hear me?" Slowly the poor man opened his eyes. "Bennings, are you alright?"

"I think so, sir." His voice was weak. Hazel noticed a very bad cut on his head.

She grabbed a towel and started wrapping it around his head. "What happened?"

"It was Miss Laura. She was very angry. We were in the kitchen and she—"

"*We?* Bennings, where is Scotty?" Hazel thought her heart was going to explode out of her chest.

"I'm so sorry, Miss Hazel. I tried to stop her. Miss Laura…took her."

John was on his feet racing for the door. He turned around and Hazel almost knocked into him. "Call 911. I'll go get Scotty."

"No! She's my baby! I'm coming!"

"Hazel, I swear to you I won't come back here without her, but Bennings needs help now. I will deal with my sister, but if we both go, it may push her over the edge. Please, darling, call 911 *now*."

Hazel was hysterical, but there was no other choice. She knew he was right—John was the only one capable of reasoning with Laura. The woman's pride was injured. On some level, John had sincerely hurt Laura. But taking Scotty was going too far.

What in the hell had gotten into her?

Chapter Twenty-One

John ran outside. It didn't take long to find Laura. He could hear Scotty screaming, and her pitiful voice led him quickly to the dock.

As he approached Laura's boat, he could hear her pleading with Scotty to be quiet. The tiny girl was huddled in the back of the boat, covering her head and weeping. Laura was standing on the shore, trapping the girl so that if she tried to flee from Laura, she'd have to swim for it.

He also noted Laura's tone—it was the tone of a woman who was quickly losing her patience. "You little brat, stay still."

"I want my mommy!" John saw Scotty poke her head above Laura's hands in defiance—and in horror, he watched as his sister slapped her across her face.

"Laura! What the hell are you doing?"

He saw his sister's body go rigid. "Goddamn you!"

"Laura, let the girl go."

"Get away from the boat, John! Or I'm taking you with us!"

There was water seeping into the bottom of the boat. "Laura, what did you do?"

"John, get away from me!" There was a pistol in her hands.

"Did you shoot out the bottom of the boat? My God, Laura—get the kid out!"

"John, I want my mommy!" The frightened and tiny voice was killing him.

Laura steadied the gun in her hand—and John saw that it was aimed right at him.

"Don't worry, sweetheart. Everything's going to be alright." He wanted to soothe Scotty, but he knew the end of this ordeal wouldn't be clean. He was going to have to make a terrible decision. He watched the water continue to fill the boat. He knew it was going to have to be a fast decision.

"Laura, I'm begging you. Let me get Scotty out of the boat. In fact, why don't all three of us go back inside the house? All three of us, Laura. And we can talk."

"You broke my heart! You picked *her* and that brat over me! I'm your blood, John!"

"I know you are, Laura. It's just that sometimes you make me very, *very* angry. That doesn't mean I don't love you anymore."

He saw the hopeless look on her face. He didn't fully understand what had transpired the last few years to cause her to do something so despicable. But his fear for Scotty overruled his worry for Laura.

"Laura, I'm going to count to three. If you don't back away from the boat and put the gun down, I'm going to have to force you—"

"Go away, John! Go inside and fuck your victim!"

"One."

"I'm not playing your game, John! You can't control me!"

"Two."

"Stop counting! Stop counting!" her voice shrieked, and he saw the hand gripping the pistol begin to shake.

"Three."

He slammed his fist over her hand, and she dropped the gun. He kicked it into the water and shoved her away from the boat. Scotty was screaming, but he managed to reach inside and grab her.

"No!" Laura reached back and bit John's arm.

He pushed her head back and slammed it into the dock. Her body went limp, and he felt the side of his face damp from Scotty's tears. He wrapped both arms around her tightly, still hearing her muffled weeping. From down the river, he could hear a rescue boat's sirens. Hazel had called 911. Soon there would be help—if it wasn't too late for Bennings.

He slowly started walking back to the house. Hazel was running toward them. He would put Scotty in her arms and deal with—

"I can't believe you are just going to leave me!"

His sister's shrill scream nearly made him jump. "Laura, stay there! We can talk about this." But she was already on her feet and running—running to the veranda—and then she vanished out of sight.

He didn't understand why Laura had tried to commit such a vile act. He sat in silence as the EMTs worked on Bennings, who appeared to be okay, other than a likely concussion. He would spend the night at the hospital.

Two policemen had accompanied the rescue boat. Upon hearing what Laura had almost done, they canvassed the property.

"Mr. Stonem, we haven't found any sign of her on the grounds, but her boat capsized an hour ago," the older officer said gently. "If you don't mind, sir, we'd like to take our search to the river for now. From what you described, your sister might have done something desperate."

John barely heard the man. His eyes and thoughts were on Hazel, who was clutching Scotty. He was relieved when the policemen left. And then it was just the three of them. After all the chaos, he needed her. Whether she was angry at him—and rightfully so—or not, he needed her.

"Is she asleep?" he whispered.

"Yes." But Hazel made no move to put Scotty down. "Did you call the hospital?"

"I did. Bennings is stable. It was what the EMT suspected: a concussion, along with a minor laceration on his head."

"We should pack some fresh clothes for him." He noted the weariness in her voice. He knelt down next to where she was cradling Scotty on the couch.

When he reached for her, he saw Hazel's grip tighten on the little girl's blanket. "I don't want to take her upstairs yet."

"I wasn't going to do that. I just want to hold her too."

She didn't object when he slid on the couch next to her and very gently scooped the little girl in his arms. Anger jolted inside of him when he saw the bruises and swelling on Scotty's face and arms. Laura had probably forced the girl to the boat, kicking and screaming.

The night could have ended an entirely different way. Instead, for at least that moment, he was sitting with the woman he loved and the child he wished were his.

"How did you know something was wrong, Hazel?" That question had been rattling his mind since he recovered Scotty.

"What?"

"You darted down the stairs. Did you hear something? Did you hear Scotty scream?"

He watched as Hazel took a deep breath. "I saw that woman again. I saw her standing by the stairs. She was holding Scotty's doll. Then she dropped it down the stairs."

He wasn't sure what to say, but he could tell she was waiting for him to make a judgment, as he had the other times she claimed to see the woman.

"I wasn't going to tell you any of that. But I'm tired of all the secrets. I'm tired of all the lies. Are you going to tell me again that it's all in my head?"

John sighed. "Whatever or whoever prompted you to run downstairs, you saved Bennings and Scotty." He heard her choke back a sob. "I am so sorry, Hazel. For all of this. Please believe me. I will *never* hurt you or Scotty again. I will—"

"John." He stared into her brilliant, golden eyes. "I don't want to be alone anymore."

He put an arm around her and pulled her close. "Then stay with me."

"I can't," she whispered.

"I'm in love with you. I don't know how to stop, or if I even can. I only know that last week, Bennings made a bold move, and however wrong he was and I was for covering it up, he brought you to me. And now I can only say that I'm sorry that I'm not sorry enough. Because in finding you, I found something I thought I had lost."

"Your mind?"

"My humanity." He turned to kiss her forehead. "I've spent all my life mourning Alison. I've wasted so much time. I could have been doing more with my life. Or at least recognized that my own sister needed serious help."

"John, listen to me. Laura is not your fault. We make our own choices. Laura is an adult. She tried to kill my child and Bennings tonight. I just thank God you saved Scotty."

"But if I hadn't trapped you—"

"Yes, you lied to me. Yes, Bennings's devotion to you is a little bit over the edge. But once I understood why, I understood that neither of you were out to hurt me. You were lost. Bennings was trying to save you."

He groaned. "Would you like to be my attorney when this goes to court?"

"John, I can forgive you because I can't leave you feeling more guilt and anguish."

And there was that word: *leave*. She was going to leave him. And why not? Her daughter's life had been endangered twice—not to mention her own life.

And John would be alone again. Alone in Alison's house.

But this time he would not let the ghosts of his past take hold. This time he would live—because Hazel was going to live, and so was Scotty.

"I'll take her upstairs," he said blankly.

He heard the soft footsteps of Hazel behind him on the stairs. The house was so quiet.

The hallway to the fourth floor was lit up. And for the first time in a long time, the air was lighter and friendlier. The dark cloud that had weighed on the soul and drenched itself inside the house had dissipated.

As he tucked the little girl in bed, he turned to see Hazel standing in the doorway. "I'm sure you're exhausted. I'm exhausted myself. If you're alright, I think I'll go to bed."

But she didn't move to let him pass. Instead, she put a hand to his chest. "John," she whispered, "I need you."

He looked at her, puzzled.

She filled in the blanks. "You read my notepad. You know my thoughts. I. Need. You."

Chapter Twenty-Two

In the past two days, Hazel's life had been flipped upside-down again, and her daughter had almost been taken from her forever. Suddenly life—real life—was dangling in front of her.

The night she and John had almost made love haunted her. It wasn't fear or hesitation or surrender that propelled her in this moment. It was *need*. She needed John. She *wanted* John. And in her heart, she felt something for John.

"Hazel."

"Shhh." She put her fingers to his lips. She didn't want to talk about Laura, Alison, or anything really. "I want to feel you against me."

He slid his arms around her. "Are you sure?"

She answered him with a kiss. A deep, hungry kiss that revealed so much longing and need that had Scotty not been sleeping just feet away, he would have satisfied both of them right then and there.

She broke the kiss abruptly. "The house is locked up?" she whispered in his ear.

"Yes," he answered, and then seized her mouth again.

He led her through his bedroom and into the master bathroom. Gold tiles and a walk-in shower fit for a king made Hazel groan. John walked into the shower, turning the water on. Steam rose from the cold tile floor.

She watched as he began stripping. First was his shirt, which he flung over his head. Then he was unbuckling his belt while kicking off his shoes. He leaned over to remove his socks and push down his jeans. Then the boxers—the last article of clothing that remained— were tossed aside. He stood naked and sublimely erect as he stepped under the hot water.

The sight of his body made Hazel unravel. She kicked off her sandals and walked into the shower. Hot water ran over her. She could feel John's hands on her. He was unzipping the back of her dress, his hands cupping her behind tightly.

She looked up at the water falling above her. It mesmerized her. For a second, she thought maybe she could freeze the moment. Scotty was safe and sound and in bed. John was in love with her. And she was feeling something she had never experienced before.

She was in love.

Tears billowed down her cheeks. There was so much water, John didn't notice. She didn't want him to notice.

Was this bliss? Was this what she had been avoiding her entire life?

His fingers peeling her dress down her shoulders and arms brought her back to the moment. He knelt before her as he pushed the fabric past her hips and down her thighs. He paused to grip her underwear, peeling the wet material off with her dress. He traced her legs and buttocks with his hands before leaning in and kissing her lower lips.

Hazel thought she would collapse from the sensation. John was gently pushing her into the corner of the shower. "You are so beautiful," he murmured. Her back against the tile, he pushed one leg up onto his shoulder and slid his tongue between her lower lips.

Her fingernails were like claws in his shoulders, but her whimpering turned to moaning, and he knew he had her. He couldn't get enough of her. He couldn't taste her enough. He couldn't feel her quiver enough. And then he felt her break. She let out a heavy moan, and collapsed against him. Her lower body was still convulsing as he slowly stood up.

She was still panting as he reached around and unhooked her bra, sliding it off of her. "John…"

He grinned wildly and began lightly pinching her nipples. She was so beautiful, so luscious, and he was dying to claim her. "Are you ready for me?"

She stared at his aching cock. She had denied him before. This time, though, she would give herself wholly to him. "John, please. Don't make me wait any longer." There was no hesitation in her voice.

Still pressing her against the tile, he picked her up, spread her legs, and let his cock find her. "I love you." He took her urgently. Each thrust kept her pinned in the corner.

"I love you." He said it again, still mad with desire and madly in love.

For Hazel's part, she couldn't get enough of him inside her. That first thrust—that first breach of her threshold—she wanted to scream his name. She wanted to cry at the relief from the bitter loneliness she endured for years—hell, most of her life. Mostly, she wanted to latch onto him forever. The intensity of his body was making her come alive with need.

John let out a growl as he came inside her. Years of hurt and rage were quieted.

She freed him.

+++

They were both still completed soaked from the shower, but John carried Hazel to the bed and tossed her on top of the duvet. She giggled like a teenager as he climbed on top of her.

"I have something for you." He winked teasingly and rubbed his already erect cock against her thighs.

In an instant, she pushed him off of her and pinned him to the bed. She knew John could overpower her, and in truth, she wouldn't mind if he did. But she also wanted the chance to explore his body.

There was a particularly stricken-looking part of him that she was eager to explore.

John clutched the pillows behind him as Hazel's tongue traced over the shaft of his cock. When her entire mouth took him in, he thought he might punch his fist through the headboard.

"You're killing me," he sighed.

Up and down her head bobbed, and the sensation of her rhythm pushed him further and further to the edge.

"Damn it, Hazel!"

He forced himself up and grabbed her. The way she looked at him—needy and desirable as hell—was all it took. He pinned her down and thrust deeply, mercilessly, inside of her.

"John!"

He couldn't stop. He lost control in raw lust, as if the world would end in the next heartbeat. "You are mine," he grunted.

She sunk her fingernails into his back and shrieked. He poured his seed into her, still cradling her underneath him, still unwilling to withdraw.

They lay in silence for several minutes, both out of breath, both entwined in one another—it was a bond John hoped would never be broken.

He bent his head down by her ear and mouthed his madness for her—he was too afraid to speak it. He was too afraid it would scare her away.

"You're an animal," she whispered, finally breaking the silence.

"I meant for this all to be romantic. Not so primal."

She giggled at him girlishly. "Oh, you *meant* all of it. I have no doubt about that."

He pulled her against his chest. "You bring out the beast in me."

John noticed as Hazel grew more and more quiet. He worried that she was having regrets. In fact, that mere notion terrified him. "Are you alright?"

She nodded and rested her head against his chest.

"Nothing was too rough? Too fast?"

She shook her head *no*.

"I didn't hurt you?"

"No, you didn't hurt me."

He doubted that to an extent. Mother or not, Hazel hadn't had sex in a very long time. Her body's tightness and her initial apprehension as he entered her told him as much. Even if she hadn't been hurt during their lovemaking, she would surely be sore.

But the bigger issue—if she was having regrets—troubled him. "Hazel—"

"John, I don't want to talk about this." Her smile alleviated much of his stress. "I don't want to stop doing this either."

She pushed him onto his back and climbed on top of him.

"Alright," he said as he ran his hands over her stomach and breasts. Sitting astride him, she looked like a goddess. Hair in waves over her shoulders. Golden eyes shimmering at him. And a body he couldn't get enough of.

As she pushed herself against his cock, he saw the haze of desire flash across her face. "This is what I want, John. To feel you inside of me again."

She pressed down. He let out a long moan.

When he opened his eyes, she was smiling down at him. "Hazel, azelHaif you don't do something, I may die."

She giggled again. "I'm not quite done with my revenge yet." Her voice was like a purr. And her rhythm was his heaven.

Chapter Twenty-Three

How many times had they made love? Hazel lost count. She only knew by the light trickling through the curtain in John's bedroom that it was morning.

He was awake and she knew he was watching her. She didn't have to turn around to know that. His half-erect cock was pressing against her back, and his hands were caressing her neck and shoulders.

She was exhausted; she was revitalized. The entire night with John had been like nothing she had ever experienced before. He was insatiable. He was completely fixated on her.

A horrific thought entered her mind: If this was all-consuming love, she suddenly understood why John had spent so many years grieving for Alison.

She had never experienced this degree of love with a man before—she had never known it even existed. And now that she did, she didn't want to let him go.

John had been right. She had lived her entire life without ever truly being in love. And now she was. She had been wrong to mock his relationship with Alison. Only now, she was even more jealous of it.

Tears threatened her newfound feelings of joy. And she chastised herself for being so foolish.

A better woman would be able to handle this.

Nothing got by John.

"What's wrong, my love?"

Even the sound of his voice was different. It was no longer John the would-be kidnapper's voice, but the voice of the man who had changed her life in every conceivable way.

It was the voice of the man she had fallen in love with.

"Nothing's wrong." She bit back tears. *Just tell him you love him.*

"Hazel, no more secrets." He was kissing her shoulders. She wanted him to be inside her again.

"Mommy!"

The urgent footsteps of her child startled her. The bedroom door was flung open. Reality returned.

Hazel grabbed the comforter and pulled it up to her neck. John leaned back against the pillows, his nether region thankfully covered. But it annoyed the hell out of Hazel that he was so calm about Scotty walking in on them.

"Hi, baby. I'm so sorry. Mommy stayed in bed too long."

She was *mortified*. She was also relieved that Scotty had bounced back from last night's ordeal with Laura so quickly.

"Is Benny home yet?"

She was ashamed that she had spent all night with John, never sparing a worry for her child and Bennings.

"No, sweetheart. But you, me, and Mommy are going to pick him up from the hospital this afternoon." Scotty clapped her hands in delight. Hazel wanted to crawl farther under the covers.

"Mommy, can I have a Pop-Tart?"

She felt John shifting his weight to the side of the bed. "How about I get you your Pop-Tart and we let Mommy sleep a little longer?"

"Okay!"

"You better get dressed first, Scotty," Hazel chimed in.

The girl skipped out of the bedroom and down the hall.

"Is it wrong that I think my child weird for not thinking anything of finding me in bed with a man?"

She watched John pull a pair of boxers out of the drawer next to the bed. "Maybe seeing us in bed gives her a sense of security."

"Oh?"

"Don't panic, but I think your child already has it in her head that I'm the daddy figure."

"That much I know." And in truth, Hazel didn't hate the idea of John being the father in Scotty's life. Scotty was crazy about John.

"So now what do we do?"

"I'm going downstairs to try and find a Pop-Tart. You're getting some rest."

"That's not what I mean, John—"

"I know. But we don't have to rush into anything, Hazel. We can just take today as today and see what tomorrow brings. The past couple of days have been horrific. The only good thing about yesterday is you being in my bed now."

She wasn't arguing with any of that. John was right. Getting Bennings back home was the priority. Assuming Laura jumped into the river, the police would find her or her body soon, and they could put the horrendous ordeal to rest.

There was plenty of time to sort everything out with John.

Hazel slowly pulled herself out of bed. The soreness was also unlike anything she had ever experienced.

"Not staying in bed?"

She looked over to see John already fully dressed. "I think I'll take a long, hot bath."

"I may join you later."

She smiled. He winked mischievously before going downstairs.

+++

John wasn't entirely sure what the hell Pop-Tarts were, but Scotty managed to talk him into ice cream instead. And why deny her? The poor girl had been through a terrible ordeal, no thanks to his family. If Scotty wanted ice cream for breakfast every day for a year, she'd get it.

Then a pang of doubt hit him. If Hazel was still intending on leaving at the end of the month, he wouldn't see Scotty every morning. Or even every day.

The realization of how close he came to losing Scotty the night before had shook him to the core. He loved that spirited little girl. He may not have fathered her, but he wanted to raise her…with Hazel.

Then an idea—an obvious idea—struck him.

"Scotty." He watched as the little girl cocked an eyebrow at him. Her face was covered with ice cream. "What if I ask your mommy to marry me?"

She smiled brightly. "Okay!" she squealed.

"Now, let's keep this a secret, alright? We need to pick out a ring for her first."

"Okay!" she squealed again. "And then you'll be my daddy?"

Even the word struck his heart: *daddy*. "I'll always be here for you, Scotty. No matter what your mommy's answer is."

And he meant it.

If Hazel said no…he didn't want to consider that. He didn't want his world to fall apart again. He spent decades mourning. Now it seemed everything he ever wanted was within his grasp.

"John?" The little one beside him also nudged his arm.

"Yes, Princess Scotty?"

"Can we live somewhere else?"

Her question puzzled him. "I thought you liked this house. I thought you liked all the toys and all the space—"

But she was shaking her head. "Me and Benny don't wanna live here anymore. That bad lady made it yucky."

"You mean Laura? Because she tried to hurt you?" He could hardly blame the girl considering what she'd been through.

"Why's that lady so mean?"

"Well, she-she has a hard time trying to form bonds—" What was he trying to do? Explain Laura's pathology to a four-year-old? "She's just sick, sweetheart. She didn't know what she was doing." He paused, and then added, "But that doesn't make what she did to you or Bennings okay."

"She's a bad lady, John. And I don't want us to live here anymore."

He considered her statement. It sounded very ominous coming from such a small voice.

On the other hand, the entire house had been built for Alison. It hardly seemed appropriate to ask Hazel to marry him *and* insist that she live in the house that essentially imprisoned her. It didn't help that Alison's pictures were all over the walls upstairs either.

John felt a rush of hope flood over him. Hazel did feel something for him. He would just have to show her how much she meant to him.

+++

Hazel carefully sat down in her bath. It was the same tub she had sunk into her very first day in the house. In many ways, she was just as sore as that day as well—yet this was a frighteningly different sensation.

John had conquered her body—no, she had given it willingly. The care he took in pleasuring her scared the hell out of her. No man had ever made her feel so desired. No man had ever made her so undone.

So much for her hopes of escaping somewhere tropical at the end of her thirty-day containment. John was right where he had planned to be: in her arms and in her heart.

She groaned, shifting her attention to the plated window near her. The weather was turning sour. Sleet and ice were falling hard.

Their chances of getting into town by boat to retrieve Bennings now looked very slim.

Poor Bennings. The man had been wrong in luring her to the house, but she could well understand his intentions, however wrong they were. And, anyway, Scotty adored him. She had to forgive Bennings for his part in this crazy situation. Laura was another matter.

If Laura was alive, Hazel *would* press charges. She would do everything possible to make sure Laura went to jail. The woman was dangerous. If Hazel ever laid eyes on that lunatic again, she wasn't sure she'd be able to control her anger. Anyone who raised a hand to her child should be very afraid.

+++

John anxiously wandered the abandoned second and third floors of the house. The rooms were typically occupied by the staff members who were still on holiday. He stopped and opened each door, and every time he found an empty room, he breathed a sigh of relief.

The weather had grown worse as the afternoon progressed. John phoned the hospital to let Bennings know they were snowed in—or iced in, as it were. The kind old man only requested that John give Scotty strict orders to have the laundry sorted by the time he returned.

After Scotty ate breakfast, she had gone back upstairs to harass her mother. John had watched as Hazel played with the girl, and read her story after story. At one point, he saw Hazel nod off, which is when he took the opportunity to patrol the house—and be alone with his thoughts.

What had Laura been thinking?

He was completely consumed with guilt and confusion. His own sister nearly killed the child he was growing to think of as his own. Had Laura succeeded, he would have lost Scotty forever. And Hazel's life would be in shambles—as his once was. It was suddenly so agonizingly unfair. Although he was in love with Hazel, he had twice caused her child harm—and it could have easily been much worse.

How could Hazel love him? How could she possibly want to stay with him after all this? Yet he knew he had to risk it and ask her to marry him. He knew if he didn't that it would haunt him forever. This was his chance. His last chance!

He breached the fourth floor. Hazel and Scotty might still be napping, but he would wake Hazel. He would talk to her about their future. And no matter what her answer was, he would accept it.

But before he could get to Scotty's bedroom, he saw the girl standing in the hallway. Her face was directed toward the open doorway of an empty room.

Chapter Twenty-Four

"Yes. I know. I like that, too."

John stopped in his tracks. Scotty was clearly having a conversation with someone, but something about the scene seemed…off. Unnatural.

"I love to swim! My nana taught me."

It was odd—odd the way he couldn't just run to her and see who or what it was she was talking to.

"I won't tell them. I can keep a secret." The girl was whispering now. And he noticed how she was taking baby steps into the room.

Urgency overruled his fear, and he finally interrupted. "Scotty?"

She jerked her head toward him.

"Whom are you talking to?" He watched as she grinned at the doorway, and then skipped toward him. He scooped her up in his arms and wondered if she could feel his heart pounding. "Who were you talking to, Scotty?"

He saw the confusion in her eyes.

"I always talk to Mrs. Winkles."

"Mrs. Winkles? Your doll?"

"Yep. Mrs. Winkles knows *everything*."

He smiled, already feeling his heart return to normal. The girl was lonely, no doubt. She was just talking to her doll.

He put Scotty down and watched as she skipped down the hall to wake Hazel. He almost followed. Almost. But for his own peace of mind, he walked into the room Scotty had been so interested in.

And he saw Mrs. Winkles—propped up against a window.

It was a peculiar sight. The doll was innocent looking enough, he supposed. Two blonde braids, big blue painted eyes, a red dress, and painted on socks. But her position against the window—the way one arm was stretched out, as if reaching for help. It troubled him. Deeply.

He was quiet during dinner. Hazel met his eyes several times, but Scotty was busy rambling off a list of things she wanted to get for Bennings. A new TV, roller skates, fabric softener, and ice cream cake. Scotty could talk forever.

He was relieved when Hazel insisted the little girl take a bath and go to bed after dessert. It was a family ritual he had never before experienced. He listened from Hazel's bedroom as she sang to her daughter, splashed the water around her, listened to the girl's nonsense stories and played along. There was a loving innocence to it all.

Which was in sharp contrast to the feeling of his house, which was so ominous. So unwelcoming.

For decades, he'd lived on Alison's memories, and he believed the house—of her taste and design—would nourish his broken heart.

Then last night had happened. When he and Hazel united, the house had felt warm and airy and free. But now…now the house had taken on an entirely different atmosphere.

+++

"You're very quiet tonight." Hazel shut Scotty's bedroom door carefully. It had taken over an hour to lull her child to sleep.

"It's been a busy day."

"A busy few days."

She noted the eerie tone in his voice. "Is something wrong, John?"

"I was thinking about Laura earlier. I was wondering if she's—"

"—been found?" She knew John well enough to see the guilt he felt.

"Yeah."

"Let's not rush to any conclusions. She may be taking refuge nearby." Though in Hazel's heart, she admitted she wouldn't be shedding any tears for Laura if and when she was found.

"I just don't understand what happened to her."

"John, don't take this the wrong way, but she's completely out of her damn mind."

He cocked his eyebrow in amusement. "And I'm so sane?"

"At least your strained sanity made sense. You lost your wife."

"You're making excuses for me."

"Maybe." Her voice cracked. His eyes were carefully watching her face—she had revealed too much. "I don't really know what I think anymore, John. Two weeks ago I was worried about making ends meet. Putting food on the table. Proving my mother wrong. Now I'm here. My child is giggling and happy all the time, despite your deranged sister. And you and I—" She couldn't even voice the words.

"We're lovers." He voiced them for her. "Do you regret sleeping with me, Hazel?"

"No," she answered quickly—and heard his relieved gasp. "Two weeks ago, though, I never would have dreamed we would be like this."

"Like what, Hazel?" She remembered his threatening tone when she nearly struck him over the head with a candlestick. She remembered how dangerous he seemed.

And now he was kneeling before her, subservient, and his deep blue eyes were pleading for an answer.

"I hated you, John. You scared me." She saw the defeat building in his eyes. "But I've never felt more alive than when I am with you. And as wrong as my head tells me that is, my heart still wants you—still wants *us*."

He didn't wait another moment to seize her.

His lips burned her like fire when they clashed with hers. He groaned as her fingers pressed along the opening of his pants, and as she slid her fingers down his zipper. In response, he grabbed the top of the dress she wore and ripped it open to her waist. She gasped in a frenzy as his mouth dipped, suckling one aching nipple as he tore the rest of her dress away.

There was nothing gentle about their joining. He pushed her to the ground, spread her legs, and buried his cock so deeply inside of her it was as if the very thrusts were claiming her. *Mine, mine, mine.* No matter what happened next, in that moment, she belonged to him.

She felt him come inside of her and squeezed her thighs tighter around him. There were bruises on her hips from their all-night encounter, and she felt fresh ones forming already. She was shocked at how powerful he was—and at how madly she craved him.

Hazel put on a robe before climbing into bed with John. She was afraid Scotty would wake up early and barge in on them again.

John looked exhausted. "We'll see what the water looks like tomorrow," she heard him mumble.

"What?"

"So we can pick up Bennings."

"Oh, right. Of course." She was embarrassed. The man was worried about his poor butler, and Hazel was daydreaming about him taking her again.

Her hopes were built up further when she felt his arms slide around her waist, pulling her closely against his body. Then his lips were nuzzling her neck. "Does Scotty do alright in a boat?"

Again, her thoughts were in a primal place. "Oh, I don't actually know." She wasn't even sure if Scotty had ever been on a boat.

"If you'd rather stay here with Scotty, I can go into town and get Bennings."

"You are not leaving me here alone in this house."

"Of course. We'll all go together."

She was relieved. Then she was suddenly very worried. How many times had she and John made love? She couldn't remember. But a total of zero times had they used a condom.

Oh God! What if she was pregnant? John made it clear he always wanted children, but she was suddenly very certain of one thing: She couldn't raise a baby in this house. If John wanted a future with her, it couldn't be in this house. And pregnant or not, she would have to convince him to leave it behind.

+++

"Mrs. Winkles and I want to go ice skating today."

"No can do, kiddo. The river is still frozen, but the temperature is warming up."

John was attempting a rather lackluster breakfast of toast and juice. He had hoped the river would have thawed, but it looked like it would be another day before Bennings could be retrieved.

"Did you call the hospital yet this morning, John? Is he alright?"

The way Hazel pronounced his name was enchanting. He was a grown man, yet he suddenly felt like a schoolboy. "I talked to Bennings this morning. He's fine—he's giving the candy stripers hell. They must be dying for us to pick him up."

"Speaking of which, I've been meaning to ask: Won't it take several hours to get to St. Jerome by boat?"

He heard Hazel's question, but he was suddenly watching Scotty very closely.

"Maybe two hours," he answered absently.

"Two hours in the cold. Do you think we should get a hotel room? Or maybe even stay in my apartment?"

He didn't answer Hazel. He was too busy watching as Scotty climbed out of her chair, holding tightly onto Mrs. Winkles. The way the girl kept looking at the doll and nodding her head disturbed him.

Scotty pushed a chair over to the window and then climbed on top of it. It was a strange sight—the little girl and doll both facing the window. Scotty was completely frozen.

"John? Did you hear me?"

He did, but he still didn't answer her. "Scotty, what are you looking at?" He rose from the table and stepped behind the little girl.

"Mrs. Winkles is upset."

Hazel was suddenly standing next to him. "What's going on?"

"Scotty, why is Mrs. Winkles upset?"

Scotty merely pointed her finger out of the window.

Hazel gripped John's hand. "What do you see, Scotty?"

"Mrs. Winkles sees the bad lady in the garden. I don't like that lady."

Hazel let out a strangled gasp.

John acted quickly. He grabbed his coat and the rifle out of the safe and made sure every door and window on the first floor was locked and secured.

"John, what are you going to do?"

He wasn't entirely sure. He hadn't seen anyone in the garden, nor had Hazel. But Scotty had been insistent. He had a gut feeling that the girl was right.

"I'll call the police again. Let's let them handle it."

"The river is still frozen, Hazel. I don't even know if emergency crews could make it. Stay in the house and lock the back door."

"John—"

"She's my sister, Hazel. I'll handle this." He was masking his panic with an angry tone, but he didn't care at the moment. If Laura really was in the garden, he was going to confront her. And if she made any more threats against Hazel or Scotty, well, he would have to take action.

The air outside was chilly, but warmer than the past few days had been. He moved quickly while trying to be as quiet as possible. The path to the garden was short, and when he reached the veranda, terror swept over him. Fresh footsteps were easily evident in the snow. They were small. Likely a woman's.

He stepped down off the veranda and started down the path through the garden. The footsteps stopped abruptly at the river. He turned and faced the house again. Could she have doubled back and entered the house? There was no hiding place that would conceal his sister—unless she was somehow utilizing the river.

"Laura?" he called.

The wind was calm. Dead silence was in the air. It was a foreboding he knew all too well. It was time to take Hazel and Scotty and leave the house forever.

+++

"This is John Stonem. My guests and I are stranded on my property and in desperate need of rescue. My boat is not sufficient enough to cut through the ice on the river. Are there any emergency crews in the area?"

Hazel was rocking Scotty in the study and listening to John call for help—any help. He hadn't seen Laura, but Hazel could tell he no longer felt safe in the house. It would have been a comfort to her if she wasn't so terrified about his sister.

"Nine o'clock this evening. We'll be ready." She heard him hang up the line.

"Are you sure this is necessary, John?"

He nodded to her and then immediately began pulling coats out of the closet.

"It's not even noon yet, John. We have plenty of time." She needed to talk to him alone. "Scotty, will you go put your toys back upstairs?" The little girl scampered off. "John, you're basing all of this on the words of a child and her doll."

"Hazel, I saw the footprints in the snow."

"But it could be—"

"One of us? Then why was there only one set? Did you take a walk out there alone this morning? They were too big to be Scotty's."

She wasn't going to argue with him. She should be relieved that they were leaving the house as she had wished. "Where will we go?" She spoke the word *we* without realizing what she had just implied.

"Wherever we want to go."

"And what about Bennings?"

"We'll pick him up from the hospital and figure it out."

"John?" She wanted him to face her. She wanted him to comfort her. She was getting more and more nervous watching him pace around the house. He finally met her gaze. "What's going to happen now?"

She felt like collapsing against him when he gathered her in his arms. "We'll get away from here. We'll start a life somewhere else."

"But how will I explain to people where I've been? And how we ended up together?"

He winked at her. "Tell people whatever you want. Tell them you fell into the clutches of an old butler and his madman employer." He was teasing her, trying to ease her tension. "Hazel, just be with me. We'll figure out the rest later. Let's just get packed and get out of here."

Scotty came bouncing back into the study holding Mrs. Winkles. John patted them both on the head before heading upstairs.

"Where are you going?"

"I'm going to grab a few last things."

"We still have several hours, John."

"Then we'll be ready several hours ahead of schedule."

+++

Upstairs, he paused in front of Alison's bedroom. For so many years it had been a shrine, meant to preserve her very essence. Now when he stepped inside the bedroom, he felt like a stranger.

Her clothes. Her knickknacks. The remnants of the time they had together. It was all bottled up like a time capsule.

Everything he had done as a young man had been for her. Everything he had done as a grieving widower had been in her name. And now he was letting her go.

"Alison," he whispered toward the vanity, where he had so often watched her put on her makeup. "I've always loved you and I always will. Please forgive me. I can't come back here after I leave tonight. I can't keep living in these walls, praying that I'll see some ghostly apparition of you. Please forgive me. Please let me go."

The softest scent of lavender filled the room. For a moment—just a fleeting moment—he thought she would appear. Instead, a warm feeling of peace stretched out over him. He wasn't sure if what he was feeling was real or fabricated by his mind. But it was enough for him to walk out of the room and shut the door. It was enough for him to move on.

+++

Scotty was sitting on the sofa next to Hazel. She lined up a teddy bear, a stuffed zebra, another doll, but Mrs. Winkles was curiously placed on a chair across from them.

"Is there a reason why Mrs. Winkles has been isolated from all your other toys?"

"Mommy, Mrs. Winkles is not a toy." She heard the insult in her child's tiny voice.

"I'm sorry, Scotty. Now, you have to choose. Three companions are all you can take with you. We aren't going to bring a luggage full of stuffed animals and friends onto the rescue boat."

"That's okay. Mrs. Winkles isn't coming."

"I thought Mrs. Winkles was your favorite?"

"She is, but she's not coming with us. She has to stay here."

"Oh? Why's that?"

"Because she *lives* here. Duh."

The abruptness in her daughter's voice caught her off guard. "Scotty, I know Mrs. Winkles is special to you. If you want to take her, you can."

"No, Mommy. Mrs. Winkles lives here. She looks after me and John. She's happy we're leaving tonight."

Hazel observed the doll curiously. "Why is she happy we're leaving?"

"Because that bad lady can't get us if we're gone."

Hazel pulled Scotty into her arms and turned the child to face her. "Scotty, Laura is not going to hurt us. She's not."

Scotty kept trying to turn her head away from Hazel, as if trying not to make eye contact. "Scotty, look at me—Laura is not going to hurt us. There's nothing to be afraid of."

"Mrs. Winkles," she whispered, "tells me secrets." She watched as Scotty turned toward Mrs. Winkles, as if afraid the doll was going to object to her next statement.

"What kind of secrets does Mrs. Winkles tell you?"

There was hesitation, but at long last, Scotty continued. "The bad lady did a very bad thing. She'll do more bad things if we don't leave."

Concern morphed into fear. "Bad things? Scotty, who is telling you this?"

"Mrs. Winkles."

"Scotty! Tell me who is filling your head with all of this."

The girl shushed her mother. "I'm not supposed to tell. He'll think he has to stay."

"Who would have to stay?" Then she understood what Scotty was saying, as unbelievable as it sounded. "Scotty, has Mrs. Winkles *lived* in this house for a long time?"

"Uh-huh."

She couldn't believe she was going to interrogate her own child. "Does she know John?"

"That's a secret," Scotty whispered.

"John's a secret? Or John can't know that Mrs. Winkles tells you things?"

"No—she says he can *never* know or else he won't leave and the bad lady will hurt him."

Hazel took a deep breath before asking her final question. "And does she see the bad lady?"

Scotty peered back at the doll hesitantly and then faced her mother again. "Not right now." Hazel sighed in relief. "But if we don't leave soon, Mrs. Winkles is afraid it will be too late."

Nine o'clock couldn't come fast enough.

Chapter Twenty-Five

The woman Hazel had seen in her bedroom, in the garden, dropping Scotty's doll—it had to be Alison. Hazel wasn't sure if she should tell John or not. Part of her felt compelled to tell him; part of her was worried that if she did, he'd change his mind and stay.

It scared her to death that a doll could be communicating with her child. She said nothing more to Scotty about taking the doll with them.

Hazel found John upstairs. He was in his bedroom, stuffing documents into his briefcase.

"Are you packed?" he asked when he spotted her in the doorway.

"What is there for me to pack?" Everything she wore was Alison's. She had no desire to take any of those belongings with her. "All I need is Scotty. And you."

He hugged her tightly. "Want me to start dinner?"

She nodded at him. "Just make sandwiches or something simple."

When he was almost out of the door, he turned and suggested, "Why don't you relax? Take a nap."

"Sure," she laughed, "I'll just take a nap while a crazy person is stalking the property."

"Hazel, it'll be a long and cold boat ride tonight. The house is locked up tight. We all need to try and relax until the rescue boat gets here."

She knew he was right, but that didn't keep her anxiety from building.

"Come here," he called to her. Reluctantly she followed him to her bedroom. He paused at her bed, plopping a small suitcase down. "Extra clothes, just in case we get wet on the boat," he remarked. He then led her to the bathroom, where he started filling the tub with hot water, adding bath salts—just as he had done that first night, the night her life changed forever.

"I want you to relax, Hazel. I don't want Scotty getting scared."

She scoffed. Scotty was likely already scared. She had a doll giving her dire warnings, for God's sake. "I appreciate this, John, I really do. But I—"

"No 'buts.' Just relax. I'll take care of Scotty. I promise. She won't leave my sight or be out of arm's reach for a second."

The conversation with Scotty had freaked her out, and she *was* cold, come to think of it. The thought of spending hours on a boat in winter wasn't exactly warming her up either. She began undressing, knowing that John was watching her every move. "This is just an excuse to get me naked, isn't it?"

She heard him laugh lightly. "I do enjoy the baths you take, Hazel Loveless." She rolled her eyes, but also thought he sounded sinfully erotic as he stretched out her last name into what sounded like a hundred syllables. *Lovelesssss.*

"I'll be just downstairs if you need me to scrub your back, or do anything else for that matter."

She smiled warmly as he cupped her face and kissed her. His kisses, she thought, were more of a cure than any old bath.

"Just take care of my kid." She winked.

He closed the door as he left, and she sank into the tub. Under the clear water, she could still see the bruises on her hips and thighs. She smiled to herself—and allowed herself a moment to fantasize about more occasions with John. Quality occasions outside of the creepy manor. A beach, perhaps. Or a quiet countryside. Anywhere but here.

She dove all the way under the water, letting the air bubbles push through her hair, the heat from the water soothing her temples.

She lifted her head and shoulders out of the water. A sudden chill in the air brought goose bumps across her skin. It was as if a window was open, but the one beside her was closed.

She looked to the door that led to her bedroom. John had closed it when he left. Now it was wide open.

"John?" she called, fully expecting him to answer. He didn't. "Scotty? Are you out there?"

She waited for a response, or any sound at all. There was nothing.

She continued to sit in silence. If someone was there, why didn't they answer her?

If someone was hiding, they wouldn't answer her.

Remnants of soap seeped into her eyes. It burned and was blurring her vision. She slowly lay back and dunked her head under the water again. Beneath the water, the soap dissipated. She opened her eyes.

Just above the water was a face—wearing an expression of pure terror. It was not Laura. No, it was a face very similar to her own. But the eyes were bloodshot. The skin was pasty and sallow. And the lips were blue, quivering and moving rapidly as if she was desperately trying to tell Hazel something. In the woman's hand, she was dangling what looked like a sharp piece of silver. She was dangling it over the tub.

Then one long index finger curled out in front of the woman, and it pointed straight toward the door to the bedroom. Hazel shot out of the water and turned toward the door. There was nothing there.

The woman lurking above the water was gone.

Hazel bent down to pick up a towel when a pair of hands grasped her shoulders.

Before she could scream, she was being pushed under the water. Her legs were kicking; her hands were grasping for the pair that held her under. The tub was long, though, and her legs couldn't press against the porcelain and give her leverage.

But she could kick above the water. And she did—with everything in her. She thrashed wildly, desperate to push herself out of the water. The hands on her shoulders were gripping tighter and tighter. Hazel needed air. Now!

She let go of the hands and grabbed an arm, twisting the skin as hard as she could. One hand released her. She pushed out of the water, gasping, then felt herself being pushed back down. She grabbed the arm again, twisting as she shrieked for John.

Then she was free. The hands were off of her. She gripped the side of the tub and pulled herself out. Dropping onto the floor, she coughed up water and grabbed a towel.

When sound and thought returned to her, she could hear the struggle in the next room. She could hear John calling her name.

He was screaming for Hazel to run.

She nearly slipped standing up, but managed to regain her balance. She ran to the door. John was trying to corral Laura into the corner. The woman looked wild. There were icicles at the ends of her hair. Her pants and feet looked wet, though if that was from the outside elements or the bathroom struggle, Hazel wasn't completely sure.

The door to the hallway was wide open. Laura made a dash. And that's when Hazel saw, in horror, Scotty standing in Laura's way.

+++

John heard Hazel scream. He saw Scotty in the doorway. He saw Laura running toward the little girl.

And then, suddenly, Laura stopped in her tracks.

Scotty was holding Mrs. Winkles like a shield. It was so strange—as if the entire scene had been paused. John had been in the kitchen making sandwiches when Scotty had stormed in, screaming that the bad lady was upstairs.

He told her to hide in the study and dashed up to find Hazel. He had almost been too late. He didn't even hear the struggle until he reached the fourth floor. When he saw Hazel fighting to live, he lost control. He hit Laura on the back of the head, which only stunned her long enough to free Hazel. He tried to drag her out of the bathroom, but she kicked him in the groin and was again trying to make her escape.

Only now her eyes were frozen on that damn doll. After a few more intense seconds, Laura pushed Scotty out of the way and ran down the hall.

Hazel was half hysterical as John handed her Scotty.

"Lock this door behind me," he ordered.

He stood in the hallway and waited until he heard the click of the lock. He knew Laura hadn't run downstairs. Because that's what she would expect him to think. Her target had been Hazel. And it seemed unlikely she would give up so easily.

"Laura, come out."

He didn't wait for her to answer. Instead, he started kicking open doors, beginning with Scotty's room. The room was vacant, but the window was broken. He looked down. The icy water looked deceptively calm. There was a thick leash of rope tied around one of the branches of the tree. It connected to the window ledge.

He wasn't sure how Laura had managed that climb. He was only sure that she was completely insane.

Then it occurred to him that he knew exactly where she was.

+++

Hazel grabbed a pair of sweats from John's bag. She threw on the clothes half in panic while watching her daughter, who was sitting on the end of the bed, rocking back and forth.

"Scotty, we're getting out of here, baby. I swear to you—we're getting out of here."

The girl didn't answer.

"Mommy is so sorry to have done this to you. But I'm going to get you to safety. I swear to you, Scotty! I love you more than anything else in the world." She hugged the child against her. "Do you hear me, baby?"

Scotty gave her a blank look. She was clutching her doll, and when Hazel released her, she began rocking again.

Hazel glanced at the clock. It was only six o'clock. There were still three hours until the rescue boat was due to arrive, and that was only if the water was cooperating.

Then there was the larger concern—what if John couldn't find Laura? Or worse, what if he did find her and she somehow overpowered him?

Hazel realized she needed to come up with her own plan, and fast.

She grabbed Scotty's coat and wrapped it around her daughter. "Listen to me," she whispered, "I don't know what you are going to make of the time we've spent here, Scotty. I don't know if you'll even remember this when you're my age. But whatever happens, I love you very much. Do you understand what I'm telling you?"

The girl nodded, still clutching her doll.

Hazel stood by the door, pinning her ear against it. If John found Laura, Hazel would grab Scotty, run downstairs, and try and phone for help. If Laura somehow overpowered John, Hazel and Scotty would hide. Hazel would try and surprise Laura. She would somehow get Scotty out of the house and down to the dock—where the rescue boat would arrive.

Desperation flooded her mind. She couldn't wait at the dock for three hours. Not with it being so cold. But what were the odds that they could hide in the house for three hours—without Laura finding them?

The most chilling thought of all entered her mind: What if the rescue boat was late?

Laura would have to be dealt with. If John failed, Hazel would have to succeed. Scotty's future depended on it. Hazel pressed her ear harder against the door. He could hear John calling out to Laura. She could hear his footsteps going down the hall.

"Scotty, come here."

The little girl dropped off the bed and rushed to her mother's side. Hazel picked her up and carried her to the rug—and the secret door that led to John's bedroom. The door was thankfully unlatched, and Hazel entered it cautiously. The door that led to the hallway was closed. Hazel put Scotty down and looked under the bed, behind the curtains and other rugs, and then locked the door to the hallway.

John's bed was massive. Hazel herself had a hard time climbing on top of it. Underneath the bed was enough space for a child.

"Come here, baby." Hazel grabbed extra blankets off John's bed and crawled underneath, making a nest for the child, whose gaze was fixated on the door to the hall.

When Hazel thought there were sufficient blankets underneath the bed, she crawled back out, clutching Scotty again. "Is Mrs. Winkles afraid? Is that why you're looking at the door?"

Scotty nodded her head. "The bad lady is waiting for us."

"I want you to get under the bed." She watched as her little girl crawled under. "I want you to stay here until either I or John comes and gets you. Okay?" Scotty nodded her head. "Whatever you hear, don't come out from under the bed. Stay put."

She kissed her child on the head, and then smoothed the duvet back down, blocking Scotty from view.

There was a key in the door to the hallway. Hazel snatched it. She would have a way to lock the door when she left. And a way to get back in when it was safe...*if* it was safe.

The fire in the fireplace was still burning bright, but it was the poker that Hazel was after. She gripped it tightly in her hand, and readied herself for what lay ahead.

Chapter Twenty-Six

John stood in the doorway to Alison's bedroom. The hallway was dimly lit. The room before him was dark. But he knew. He knew before his hand reached to turn on the light that she would be there.

The light exposed every inch of the room. The bed was untouched: The white comforter was perfectly pressed against every corner, the lavender pillows lined up against the headboard. A cream rug covered the floor, untarnished and unstained. The portraits on the walls were unmoved. The vanity with Alison's perfumes and makeup was untouched—other than the occupant who sat silently in the chair.

He stepped inside the room. What had once been a sanctuary he shared with his wife was now a sick shrine. It tore his heart up thinking of the years he wasted choosing to mourn rather than to live.

Alison wouldn't have wanted this.

And there was his sister—the other woman who'd broken his heart—sitting in Alison's chair.

"Why are you doing this?" He broke the silence, but she didn't move or startle at his words.

"I knew you were angry before. About me trying to commit you."

"Which time?" he snapped.

"The first time." Her voice was barely more than a whisper.

"I expected that from our father, if he were still alive. But you? My own sister. My own blood. How could you?"

"I thought you and I could get past that. I thought that eventually you would stop grieving for Alison."

"I have stopped, Laura. I'm letting go at last."

He stepped back when she abruptly rose from the chair, knocking it to the floor. "Only because *she* is here! She and that brat!"

For some reason, Laura hated Hazel. He couldn't understand that. It made more sense for Laura to hate John himself. Not a woman and child she didn't even know.

"I want you to get help, Laura. I don't want this to be your end."

"My end? Why is this *my* end? This should be *her* end—and *our* beginning!"

She was clutching her hands, digging her nails into her palms. Droplets of blood were falling onto the rug. And he knew in that moment that he wouldn't be able to talk her out of her delusion. He would have to make some awful decision quickly.

"Laura, I don't understand where this is coming from. You and Bennings looked after me for a long time. I thought you of all people would be happy for me. Happy because I found—"

"Another woman? That's why I should be happy for you? When I've spent so many years waiting for you to let go of Alison— waiting for you to be free. And this is my great, fucking reward! Watching you fawn over another woman!"

Her words were starting to sink in. He felt utterly sick. "You're my sister. And I have always loved you. But I don't like what you're saying to me right now."

He took another step back as she approached and dropped to her knees in front of him. "Don't you remember us, John?" He shook his head in defense against her pleading eyes. "We had that night together, John. That perfect night."

"What are you talking about?" His words were guttural. Bile was building in his throat.

"It was right before you left on that trip. Father's gala, remember? She fell asleep in the study afterwards. You were in here—in her bedroom. You called me over to you."

He stepped away again and hit his back against the wall. "I certainly don't remember any such night. You need help, Laura. You need *so* much help."

"I could smell the bourbon on you. But the way you touched me…I never knew such pleasure."

He pushed himself away from the wall and shoved her out of the way. He pulled back the curtains and opened the window. Never in his life had he felt so sickened. "I don't remember any of this, Laura! Tell me the truth now: Are you lying?"

There were tears streaming down her cheeks. "How could you not remember this, John? I'd never experienced that degree of—"

"Stop it! Tell the truth, Laura. Are you making this up?" She shook her head, again with her pleading, pathetic eyes. "Why would you, Laura? Why would you get in bed with me!"

"I've always loved you, John. Maybe it was wrong, but I always thought you might love me too. And then we had that night. And then…then you just…ignored me. Like it didn't happen. You picked things back up with Alison like we never had that night. You just left me behind!"

"No. No. No. Why, Laura? Why?" He felt his eyes burning. He saw the hurt in her eyes. He was outraged, stunned.

"You just carried on, didn't you? Like I didn't matter. But *she* knew. And she was going to put me away, John."

"Who knew? Are you saying Alison knew?" His heart was pounding. The horrific revelation made his whole body shake.

Her words were like bullets, each one penetrating a different part of his heart. "What did you do, Laura?" He pulled her off the floor and pushed her against the wall. "Tell me what you did. Now."

+++

Hazel stepped quietly into the hallway and closed the door to John's room, locking it. She dropped the key in the bulky pocket of her pants and stepped slowly toward the voices.

One was John's; the other most certainly was Laura's.

As she progressed down the hallway, a blast of cold air rushed through her. Suddenly her arms and legs were shaky. Goose bumps tickled up and down her body. And a shadow began to take shape in front of her.

The dress was the same. The hair was the same.

The fear did not overwhelm Hazel this time. It was as if she was expecting the woman. It was as if her entire life had been leading up to this very moment in time.

The face was clear now. For the first time, it wasn't pasty and sallow, but flesh-colored. Her lips were ruby red. And her voice, when she spoke, was calm and clear.

"You're almost out of time."

The woman slowly moved toward Hazel. She smiled warmly. With each step she took, Hazel began to feel overly emotional— overly saddened and anxious.

"I'm not afraid. I'm not." Although Hazel's voice was shaky, she meant her words.

"You were never supposed to be afraid. Not of me."

"Scotty's doll—that was you."

She nodded. "It was I who was afraid. You couldn't remember. You couldn't see." She lifted her arm slowly and pointed that long index finger at Hazel. "But you see now, don't you?"

It was no more than a touch of her finger onto Hazel's arm. But it released a flood of emotions through Hazel. Emotions of love. Emotions of betrayal. Memories that had been locked away in the heaviest vault were suddenly unleashed.

"Oh my God!" Hazel sank to her knees. Tears rolled down her eyes as her life—or someone else's life—cascaded through her mind. She was gasping for air. She was gasping for reason. And then, she stepped back into her life.

Her former life.

She was standing in a wedding dress in front of a mirror. John's mother was scornfully glaring at her while sipping her white wine. John's sister was helping pin her veil on. Laura had been so thoughtful in making sure all the flowers were arranged perfectly in the little chapel. But Mrs. Stonem remained cold as ice, certain she was a gold digger.

She didn't care about John's mother, though. Or the disdain she knew his father felt for her as well. It was all about John.

So ambitious. So loving. So hers.

The wedding bells were chiming. It was her wedding day, but it was one of the hardest days of her life. She walked down the aisle alone. She had no family, no parents. The pews on her side in the chapel were nearly bare.

Halfway up the aisle, though, Bennings stepped out of his seat, reached out to her with his arm, and she latched on. He wasn't just the butler; he was a fill-in father for John—and now for her. And then she was standing at the altar. Bennings took her hand and placed it in John's. And her love—her husband—beamed at the sight of her.

"I'm going to spend the next thirty years in bed with you," he whispered.

"Just thirty years? And then what?"

"Then I'll need a meal."

She blushed.

The minister cleared his throat awkwardly. "Do you, John Marcus Stonem, take this woman to be your wife? To love and to cherish her? In sickness and in health? Til death do you part?"

"No," John interjected. There was a slight gasp among the seated guests, and she thought she saw John's mother smile. But then John continued. "Not even death will part us." He took both her hands and squeezed them. "Say it—say that not even death will part us."

"Not even death will part us. Nothing will part us." The unity candle next to the minister ignited as if casting a spell.

And then she was Mrs. Stonem. Mrs. Alison Stonem.

Hazel was breathing heavily. She was back kneeling in the hallway—as herself, or her new self. She was listening to John's voice. His angry voice.

And the woman who had been plaguing her mind for weeks was fading away. "Now you remember. Now you know." She stepped closer to Hazel and kneeled before her. "You know what she did. You know what she'll still do." They were face to identical face.

"I don't understand. How could you be here all this time, and also be *in* me?"

The woman smiled. "Unfinished business." She opened the palm of her hand and dropped a jagged piece of silver.

Hazel knew what it was. The day she and John had driven to the property. The shiny silver all over the ground. The piece of silver before her was the piece that she had hung on the headboard of their bed. She had hung it for luck. And now it was back.

"The soul of that sunshine child was gone, and she's been at rest all this time. But we needed a place to go. *You* needed a life to live so you could finish this." The fading woman pressed her forehead against Hazel's. "And now the two halves become whole."

Hazel felt a rush of force through her entire being. The image of her other half—her former half—was gone. The silver trinket was in her hand. She clutched it tightly.

Hazel knew the truth now. Anger and fury rose up inside of her. "Save him," she said aloud and threw caution to the wind. "I'm coming, Johnny."

Chapter Twenty-Seven

"Answer me, Laura." John's head was spinning.

"That's why I married Cutter, you know." Her voice became whimsical again. "He so reminded me of you—his taut body, his lips, even his voice sometimes resembled yours."

"I'm your brother! Don't you understand how wrong this is? Don't you see how sick this is?"

"Yeah, I had those thoughts. I tried to convince myself that it was just because Mother and Father sent me away and you were the only one who was kind to me. You were always there to comfort me, to hold me—"

"As your brother! Not your lover!"

"Even Alison noticed. She told me the day you went on your trip that what you and I were doing was wrong. Like she had any right!" He noted the swift change in her voice—from whimsical Laura to damaged, angry Laura. "You were always mine, John! And when that bitch tried to tell me my place, I knew I had to act. I knew she'd try to take you from me forever."

"Laura, if you did something to her—"

"She did."

John snapped around to see Hazel standing in the doorway. She was holding a poker in one hand and a silver charm in the other.

"Oh good. It's a party." Laura snapped at Hazel, as John pushed her behind him and away from his sister.

He couldn't stand for Hazel to hear any of this. How could he possibly explain what sickened him to the very core? "Hazel, please go back to Scotty."

Defeated—that's what he was. No matter how much he loved Hazel, his past would always own him.

"I want you to tell John the truth, Laura." Her voice stunned John. He must be losing his mind.

"And what truth would that be, my dear? That he cheated on his wife?"

"Are you talking about the night you took advantage of your own brother while he was so drunk he couldn't see straight?"

"Hazel—"

"I can't let her walk away, Johnny. I know what she's done." Once again he heard that inflection in her voice. He heard her call him *Johnny*. His heart skipped a beat.

+++

Hazel saw the shock on John's face. It was nothing compared to the shock on Laura's.

"That's right, Laura. Sorry to ruin your fun, but I already know."

John looked crushed. Hazel wanted to kill Laura for hurting him so badly.

"Eavesdropping at the door? How unbecoming."

"No, Laura. Not eavesdropping. *Remembering*."

"You're bluffing. It's already been well established that you are not Alison. So stop pretending like you know everything when you—"

"I woke up in the middle of the night. I was in the study because I hadn't wanted to be with John while he was so totally smashed. I went upstairs to check on him, Laura, and I saw *you*. I saw you lying naked next to him." She glared at Laura and saw the fear in the woman's eyes. "I couldn't believe it. I knew you were a thief, but I didn't comprehend until that moment just how fucked up you really were."

"Maybe you just couldn't satisfy him."

Hazel saw John clench up at Laura's remark, but she waved her hand toward him. "I bet you were very angry he didn't remember anything in the light of day. I bet you stewed in your bedroom about it. You couldn't wait to give me every disgusting detail."

"Laura, my God!" It was killing her to hear the horror in John's voice, but the truth was the only way to save him—and the only way to save Scotty and herself.

"But you never told him, did you, perfect Alison! You never spoke the words."

Hazel looked into John's eyes. He was a shattered man. She wanted so badly to take him away from this awful scene. "No, I was never going to tell John. I love him too much to hurt him that way. He clearly didn't remember it, and you clearly were angry that he couldn't. I wouldn't shatter his world for your depraved fantasy. Still, you got your revenge, didn't you?"

+++

John was visibly shaking. He knew he was.

Laura sidled up next to him. "Don't hate me, John. I couldn't help it. I just wanted time for us to be alone together. Just some privacy. I love you, John!"

"If you loved him, you would have never put him through this. I would have spared him your awful secret forever." John wanted to run to her—he wanted to shake her and see if Hazel was playing a game. But he knew she wasn't. Her voice, her mannerisms, her memories—it was Alison. *She* was Alison.

"Alison?" He was crying openly, and he didn't give a damn what either of them thought of it.

"Johnny, you don't deserve this pain. I never wanted you to know about that night—I was prepared to move on with our life…but Laura had other plans."

He looked at his sister, who was suddenly clutching his arm as though he was her lifeline. "No, John! It's a trick—you can't listen to her. She'll say anything to save herself. She'll call the cops. They'll arrest you for kidnapping her and that brat! Bennings will spend what little time he has left in a prison cell!"

"I was sitting on the windowsill, John. I was reading. You know how I liked to read in the evenings. She was mad because I wouldn't call you and tell you about her repulsive act. She was mad because I had no intention of leaving you."

The air from the window was cool. The day had been trying— Laura had gone too far.

"John wanted me," Laura had said, and Alison slapped her hard across the face.

"John would never lust after his own sister. You tricked him."

"He called me Alison, but that was just a little game between us. And then he told me to get into bed."

She could have vomited. Yet she couldn't deny what she had seen—her own husband and Laura, lying in bed together. Naked.

"He was drunk, you fucking lunatic! What you did would ruin him if he knew—he'd never forgive himself."

"He didn't push me away, Alison. You saw that with your own eyes, didn't you?"

"He was drunk! My God, do you hear yourself?"

"Why don't you call him? Why don't you tell him? Then let him come home and decide which life he wants—one with a nagging wife, or one with a sister who loves him more than anything!"

Alison shook her head in anger. Telling John what his sister had done would undo him. It could destroy their marriage—and their happiness. And she couldn't let that happen. Not to John. Alison was the one who grew up with no one and had no one. She could survive hell. John would bury himself in guilt.

"I'm not telling John. And if you do, Laura, I swear—I'll kill you."

"You'll kill me?" John's sister was teetering on the edge of sanity.

"Or I'll have you locked up. No one would believe that John would sleep with his sister. He has an unscathed reputation, unlike you, Laura. You think about that before you open your mouth."

"I've been in John's life a long time. Don't think I'll go quietly."

She laughed. What a joke: Laura was never quiet. "You just think about what I've said before you start spreading your poison to John, or to the first reporter dumb enough to listen. If you truly love your brother, you'll forget what happened and you'll leave this house. Forever."

Laura had stormed off in a tantrum. There was nothing more to say. Either she'd say something to John, or she'd stay quiet. Regardless, Alison would find a way to get Laura out of their lives permanently. For John's own good.

At her window, Alison sat reading. The air smelled like fall. The water rushing below her sounded urgent, angry, and if she had been more logical than emotional, the warning would have been clear.

But it wasn't. A single rebel yell followed by a swift push from her sister-in-law sent her hurling out of the window and into that deep water. That deep, black water.

"I hit my head," Hazel remarked.

She saw John's eyes transfixed on her—while Laura still had one hand pathetically latched onto him.

"You hit your head?" His voice—so familiar and gentle. He was suddenly a young man again. He was suddenly so fragile to her.

"When she pushed me, I hit my head on something. Then I was in the water. It was cold." She stepped closer to John. "Then I wasn't in pain anymore."

She reached out for John, and he jerked his arm out of Laura's grasp to grip Hazel by her waist. He stared into her eyes until they were both reading what was inside the other.

"Then I was Hazel Loveless. The miracle child who woke up from a two-month coma. My mother was Beth Loveless. She worked at a diner. Then I worked at a diner." The tears were streaming down her cheeks. "I felt lost for so long, and I never understood why. When I had Scotty, I thought that was my sole purpose." She was glued to him. "Had I not seen that job listing for St. Jerome's…"

"But you did." He was kissing her hand; her trembling was subsiding. The emptiness and loneliness she had felt her entire life was suddenly being filled.

There was only one obstacle left. And she was standing in the room with both of them.

"Laura has to be stopped. She'll hurt you. She'll hurt Scotty."

"No—I won't let her." They both stared down Laura, who was backed against the very window Alison had fallen from.

+++

"We can do this the easy way, Laura." John glanced at this watch. It was ten after seven. The rescue boat was still nearly two hours away. "Or we can do this the hard way."

"What are you going to do, John? Manhandle me? Tie me up? All because that woman is playing you?"

He didn't want to listen to her. Just the sound of her voice was turning the rage inside of him to lava. He could kill her. He wanted to kill her.

"We can lock her in the study." Hazel was so wise. Hazel. Alison. Whatever she wanted to be called, he'd do anything for her.

"Good idea. There are no windows and only one door to the study." He caught her smile, but quickly turned his full attention to Laura.

His sister was seething at both of them. John moved quickly. He grabbed her arm and swung it behind her back. She struggled, kicking and slapping at him with her free hand. Hazel approached and pushed the pointed edge of the poker into his sister's abdomen. Laura stopped squirming.

"Let's go downstairs, nice and slowly." He was corralling her toward the stairs.

They began their descent. He was growing more and more anxious by the second. "Hazel?"

"I'm right behind you. If she tries anything, I'll stab her with the poker."

John could feel Laura's body grow tense, but he continued to guide her. "Slowly, one step at a time."

"Maybe I should get in front of you, John. In case she gets wild."

"Don't you come near me, you bitch!"

John squeezed Laura's arm tighter until she winced. "I said slowly, one step at a time. And keep your goddamn mouth shut."

He was suddenly daydreaming about his life. His future...with his wife. And Scotty! It was all about to come true. Laura would be secured and taken into custody. They would all pick up their lives. The way it should have always been.

He would marry Hazel, Alison, whatever she wanted to be called. They'd have a honeymoon again. They might even have more children. He could adopt Scotty. They could build another house somewhere far, far away.

His thoughts made his heart grow light. He turned around to see his wife walking so attentively behind him. It was in that moment of total love that he forgot how dangerous his sister was.

Laura abruptly halted, stomped John's foot with her own, and shoved him away from her as hard as she could. He hit the cast-iron railing of the staircase face-first, his forehead taking the brunt of the force.

Chapter Twenty-Eight

Hazel screamed as John slumped to his knees, his head smacking into the stair. She was relieved when he didn't fall all the way down the staircase, but her relief was short-lived. John wasn't moving.

But Laura was.

Hazel turned around and ran up the stairs. No matter what, she had to protect Scotty. Her anger at Laura overwhelmed any fear she might have had.

She could hear the woman trailing up the stairs behind her. Good. Leave John alone until I can get to him.

Her plan was simple. And she executed it swiftly. Back into Alison's—her—room she ran. Laura was right behind her, but Hazel ducked behind the door quickly and waited.

When Laura launched herself into the room, Hazel made her move. She flung the door closed and lunged at Laura, edge of the poker heading right for Laura's throat. Laura jumped to the side and pushed the vanity chair that was lying on the floor straight into Hazel's path. Her momentum propelled her; she tripped and fell against the windowsill. The poker dropped from her hand.

At once, she felt Laura's hands go around her throat. "I killed you once, bitch! I'll kill you again!"

Hazel was able to focus long enough to punch Laura in the throat. When Laura fell back, wheezing, Hazel grabbed the edge of the window ledge and pulled herself to her feet.

She turned back to Laura, who was already nearly recovered. "I will not die because of you and your poison. Neither will John or Scotty."

With another rebel yell, Laura charged Hazel full force. At the last second, Hazel ducked away from Laura's path. Laura crashed through the glass and went over the edge.

Hazel heard her scream—and realized that Laura was dangling outside of the window but still holding on to the ledge. "Pull me up, Hazel! Please!"

"Why should I? You let me go right over and never looked back!"

"Please! I don't want to die!"

She saw the fear in Laura's eyes. The mother in her was compassionate. She didn't want to be a murderer.

Laura had fallen too far for her to reach by hand. Cautiously, Hazel picked up the poker. "Alright, grab onto this and I'll pull you up. Don't try anything stupid."

Hazel dangled the poker down, and Laura grabbed it tightly. Hazel began pulling Laura up. But as soon as Laura was able to reach the inside ledge of the window, she grabbed Hazel with her other hand and pulled her half out of the window.

"What the hell are you doing? I'm trying to save you!"

"I don't want to be saved! John is probably dead anyway! And you know what? I'm not going alone!" Laura's grip on Hazel was deadly, but Hazel still had the poker in her other hand. In a split-second decision, Hazel slammed it against Laura's chest. Laura gazed up at her in horror, and let go of both Hazel and the ledge.

Hazel watched as Laura fell silently into that awful, black water. She never resurfaced.

Chapter Twenty-Nine

The rescue boat arrived an hour earlier than expected. Hazel had tried to phone for help after Laura's fall, but unfortunately, the boat had already been dispatched and no one was able to get to the house any faster.

The captain of the boat was called, simply, Hagen. He was an older man and in a way, he reminded Hazel of Bennings. Still, the boat ride to St. Jerome's was an excruciating two hours. Ice was forming as the temperature began to plummet, hindering their boat's progress.

John was still breathing. He wasn't conscious, but he was still breathing. There was still hope. She held John's hand while Scotty clung to her lap. Her world had just been completed; she feared it was all about to come apart.

Once the boat docked, John was loaded into a waiting ambulance. Hazel and Scotty followed in a rescue vehicle.

The hospital's emergency entrance was lit up, despite the poor weather. Hazel grabbed Scotty and followed as John was unloaded from the ambulance and rushed inside by EMTs.

Hazel wanted to follow but was instead led into a waiting room outside of the ICU. She fought back tears when she saw Bennings walking toward them. The hospital was small enough that she knew he must have seen John being rushed through the corridor on a stretcher.

"Benny!" Scotty raced to Bennings, who scooped her up as he had done a dozen times before. "I missed you, Benny!"

"I missed you, Miss Scotty! How is the laundry coming along?"

Hazel gave them their moment of reunion before she filled in Bennings on what had happened. She caught him eyeing her suspiciously.

When a doctor asked if she and Scotty wanted to be examined, Hazel jumped at the opportunity. It was enough to tire out Scotty, who fell asleep in her arms.

Captain Hagen approached her to say that the police were going to start dragging the river for Laura.

"So Laura is dead?" Bennings didn't seem exactly saddened by that possibility.

"We struggled in my bedroom. She fell from the window." Hazel paused and sipped the weak coffee served in the waiting room. "Sort of a fitting end, I guess. But I'm so worried about John."

Bennings was looking at her rather peculiarly. "Miss Hazel? Are you quite yourself?"

She held his hand in hers. "I'm fine, Bennings. It's John who's hurt. It's John who hasn't regained consciousness. And if Laura succeeded in—"

Nope, she wasn't going to finish the thought.

"Miss Hazel?" The twinkle in his eye revealed all. "Or should I say, Miss Alison?"

"How did you know?" she whispered.

"The way you hold my hand. When I'd fall off the wagon and get tremors, you'd hold my hand and sit with me until I steadied myself."

It occurred to her then that she didn't yet remember all of her former life. It was still flooding back in bits and pieces. "Laura pushed me, Bennings. It was Laura all those years ago."

"I suspected as much, but I never had proof. I only knew that Miss Laura acted very suspiciously right after it happened."

"You never told John?"

"No. He was in agony. But it was enough to make me stop drinking in truth. I wasn't as…aware as I should have been the day you died. I felt I had let Mr. John down."

"Bennings, it wasn't your fault. Laura was insane. She almost killed you. She almost killed all of us."

"I'm so relieved that little Scotty is unharmed."

Hazel looked down at the sleeping angel in her lap. "I am, too. I just wish the doctor would tell us what's going on with John. It's been hours."

"He will be alright, Miss Alison. We must have faith."

After eight hours, Hazel's patience—and faith—were gone. The doctor hadn't spoken to them. A nurse had stopped by and merely said they would get an update soon. "Soon" was hours ago.

When Hazel was about to lose her grip, a doctor finally arrived.

"I'm Dr. Weston. I need to speak with a relative of Mr. Stonem's."

Hazel nearly charged him. "You can talk to me. I'm his wife." Immediately, she regretted her words. John was the town's millionaire hermit. Everyone knew he was widowed. The doctor eyed her suspiciously. "I'm sorry. I'm Mr. Stonem's...fiancée. We were to be married right before this awful incident happened."

"Assuming you're telling the truth, the only other next of kin listed is his sister, whose body was pulled from the river this morning."

Relief—and horror—filled her mind. Remembering Scotty's presence, she glanced over at the child. But Scotty was still sitting in a chair with her earphones on, listening to a children's book on tape. *Thank God.*

"Please, Dr. Weston. Tell me what's going on with John."

"He has regained consciousness. But there's a problem."

"What is it? Brain damage?" Hazel tried to keep from going to a dark place, but she knew from experience that the longer John was unconscious, the more likely it was that there would be some major trauma.

"The optic nerve has been very badly damaged."

"So he can't see?"

"No."

She had a fleeting thought of the day John and Scotty had been playing in the snow. He was pelting her lightly; she was pummeling him to the ground. Their laughter had sparked a light within her.

How could John be blind?

"Is there a fix? A surgery? A treatment? Anything?" She knew she was sounding like a madwoman.

"The nerve is essentially crushed. There's a specialist in New York who may be able to repair the damage, but there's no guarantee Mr. Stonem will see again, not with the severity of the damage."

Tears were running down her cheeks. "Does he know he's blind?"

"He just knows something is wrong. He became agitated and we had to give him a mild sedative—just to relax him and take the edge off."

"I want to see him."

The doctor led her to the elevator. No matter what happened, she and John would be together. They would get through this. It was just one last obstacle. One last hurdle.

When the elevator opened, she could hear John. He was bossing someone around. "Stop feeding me as though I'm a baby! I'm not a goddamn invalid!"

Hazel stood in the doorway. There was a bandage over John's eyes. His face had grown stubbly overnight. There was a wildness in him. It was fear. And loneliness, too.

When the nurse again tried to feed him applesauce, he flung the tray away, spilling it and his water on the woman.

"Mr. Stonem, if you don't settle down, we will have to give you a stronger sedative." Hazel could tell she was out of patience.

"No! No needles! No restraints! You leave me the fuck alone!"

Dr. Weston was about to intercede, but Hazel pulled at his arm and motioned silently for him and the nurse to leave the room.

Reluctantly, they both left. As the door clicked shut, John kicked his legs out from under the covers.

"Shhh, they'll only leave me in here with you if you can behave."

+++

Her voice was a lifesaver. When she reached out to smooth the hair off his forehead, he wanted to weep.

"Hazel?"

"I'm right here."

"Don't leave me. I can't see."

"It's alright, John. I'm not going anywhere, but you have to calm down."

He was on the verge of an anxiety attack. He hated himself for feeling so weak and helpless, but he had no idea how long he'd been in the hospital, or where Hazel and Scotty were.

"I can't see."

"I know you can't." There was something in her voice he didn't care for: worry.

"Why can't I see? Why can't I take this damn bandage off?"

She climbed into bed with him and drew him close to her. "When Laura pushed you, you smacked your head against the railing. It damaged your optic nerve."

He gulped. "How bad is it? Can they repair it?"

"There's a doctor in New York who may be able to help. But you have to calm down and rest so I can take you out of here. You have to calm down, my love."

If he couldn't see her, how could he protect her? How could he raise Scotty? How could he be of any use?

"John," she was whispering in his ear, "I know you're scared. But I love you, and I want to be with you. Nothing else matters." Even still, he could hear her voice start to break. "Please don't give up. I just now got you back—and there's so much I still can't remember. I need you, Johnny. I need you to help me."

He held onto her. He remembered the loss he felt the last time he was in the hospital. The arms that were holding him down, injecting him with drugs to keep him calm. Today had been a horrifying reminder of that time.

This time, though, was different. Alison was back. He was holding her, touching her, smelling her. And she still wanted him and needed him.

He touched his bandage lightly, and then laughed heartily.

"What's so funny?"

"Do you remember when we fought in the kitchen? I told you that you were blind when it came to love?"

"I remember, John."

He tapped on his bandage. "Ironic, isn't it?"

+++

His laughter had returned, and she reciprocated—even though she wanted to smack him for making her laugh when moments ago she could have cried for him.

"What do you want me to call you? Hazel? Alison? Both?"

She could barely wrestle around it. Her life as Alison with John was getting clearer, and the memories, apart from Laura, were lovely. But Hazel was Scotty's mother. And despite John's many flaws in the wake of his grieving, Hazel had come to love John. And John, her.

"I'm Hazel Loveless. I have a little girl named Scotty, and I apparently fell in love with my warden slash past-life husband."

"You just said a mouthful." She laughed at his response. "I do love you, Hazel. You, Alison. Both of you. All of you."

"All of me, John. Maybe I had to be Hazel—tough girl, anti-love and anti-happy endings—in order to fix what happened in the past."

Hazel left John only after he had fallen into a deep sleep. She wanted to check on Scotty—and she figured Bennings needed a break from the nonstop chatter.

"I'll sit with Mr. John."

"Thank you, Bennings."

It wasn't until after Bennings was out of sight that Hazel realized Scotty was staring at her peculiarly.

"What's up?"

"I know a secret, Mommy." Scotty grinned.

"What secret?" Hazel wondered if Scotty was spending too much time at the hospital. She wondered if she ought to send the girl and Bennings back to her apartment.

"Mrs. Winkles is gone for good now."

"I know. You left her at John's house."

"You know what I mean, Mommy."

Hazel cocked her eyebrow.

Scotty merely winked at her mother, and then extended her tiny hand and touched Hazel's face.

"What are you trying to tell me, baby?"

The girl gave no answer, just turned her attention to the television and the obnoxious cartoon that was blaring.

It occurred to Hazel that she *did* understand what Scotty had said. Alison—the ghost of her former self—had spoken to Scotty in the most delicate way possible: through a doll. And now that Alison was…restored, there was no need for Mrs. Winkles.

Hazel sat quietly next to her daughter. On the end table next to her right was a pad of paper. She grabbed it without thought. Instead of feeling lost, she was feeling something else entirely.

Hand in hand we'll walk with our children wrapped between us.
The past is gone,
   gone, gone. The center of madness, vanquished.
Now the only thing mad is our love.

+++

John was listening to Bennings read the newspaper. Somewhere else in the city, Hazel was busy packing up her apartment. They were going to be a family.

There was just one more question John had—and he didn't want to ask Hazel.

"My sister's dead, isn't she?"

He heard Bennings clear his throat abruptly.

"It's alright, Bennings. I just want to know."

He heard the old man shuffle closer to him. "After your attack, there was a struggle between Miss Laura and Miss Hazel. Miss Hazel was almost pulled to her death by your sister but ended up overpowering her, sir. Your sister fell from the window and into the river."

"Just like what happened to Alison."

"Yes, sir. I believe that was the point. However, this time around, luck was on our side."

His sister was gone. He felt bad that he wasn't upset by the news. But the damage Laura had inflicted would haunt him forever. The last image he had seen was of Hazel standing behind him on the stairs. She was beautiful. She was his life.

He'd hold onto that image forever.

Chapter Thirty

Life had a funny way of spinning around.

A month ago, Hazel Loveless had been worried about bills and heating the apartment and keeping her job. Now she held in her hand a check for a quarter of a million dollars. John had upheld his end of the bargain.

It was Hazel who hadn't.

Movers were in and out of the manor. Barely anything was leaving with them, though. Furniture was to be donated to various charities. The paintings that John had once so adored were being auctioned off.

"Mrs. Stonem?" A mover was carrying something large and folded down the stairs.

"Yes?"

"There are about a dozen more rugs on the fourth floor. Where do they go?"

She paused to look at the one he held. Orange and gold—the one that concealed the secret door from her room to John's. She smiled to herself.

"That one will go in storage, the rest go in the auction pile."

"Yes, ma'am."

An older woman stepped through the front door. She looked worried. "Can I help you?" Hazel called.

"I'm Mrs. Thornberry, the housekeeper here. I've been on holiday for the past four weeks. What in the world is going on?"

Bennings, thankfully, interjected. "Mrs. Thornberry, this is Mrs. Stonem."

The woman looked shocked—but it was a look Hazel was getting used to. Over the past week, various employees of the estate had trickled in and out, each one giving a half-shocked and half-curious response to Hazel's presence.

"Mrs. Stonem? Mr. John's gotten himself married again?"

"Yes, Mrs. Thornberry. John and I married just over a week ago at city hall. It was a small affair—just Bennings, my daughter, and a judge. But that's all that we wanted.

"Now, Mrs. Thornberry, you may or may not have heard about John's injury. We'll be leaving for New York in a few hours to meet with a specialist and talk about surgery to correct his optic nerve. You are welcome to join us there. We'll need help settling into the apartment in the city. But we're also keeping the manor open for local tours and charity events, so plenty of staff will be needed here as well. Go or stay, it's up to you."

It was a speech Hazel had memorized and repeated too many times to count, but it seemed to do the trick. As soon as Mrs. Thornberry realized she would not be out of a job, she softened up.

"I think I'd like to stay here, if that's alright with you, ma'am."

"That will be lovely. Thank you, Mrs. Thornberry."

"If I can ask, ma'am, when will you and Mr. John return home?"

Hazel smiled brightly. "This will not be our home anymore. But you are welcome to call it your home for as long as you'd like."

Hazel went to check on John in the study. He sat listening to the news and sipping his precious brandy. She was amazed at how he could relax outside of the hospital. If the shoe were on the other foot, Hazel wasn't sure she would be as calm about her own blindness.

Their wedding had been brief, but perfect in a sense. Hazel didn't want anything fussy or larger-than-life. She'd had enough of that the first time. John just wanted her. There was no need to go to a lot of trouble, though Bennings did convince them that they should at least dress the part. John wore a casual brown suit with dark sunglasses that Bennings picked out. Hazel bought a new dress—her first one that wasn't from a discount rack. It was just a basic white dress but with unique beading around the neckline. She thought John would enjoy running his hands over the beads that curved against her bosom.

Judging from his appetite on their wedding night, he was not disappointed. Blind or not blind, John was a very thorough lover.

Bennings had tried to tell Hazel that she couldn't possibly close up their affairs and be in New York in a week, but clearly Bennings underestimated the abilities of a former single mother who could multitask like lightning.

Now it was suddenly the day they would all leave the manor. A bright and sunny day, despite the late winter coldness closing in.

"Christmas in New York this year." John's spirits were high. She hoped they stayed high. There was no guarantee where his sight was concerned.

"I know. I hope it's not too cold. I can barely tolerate this winter as it is."

"Do you know what I want to do with you in New York, wifey?"

"What's that, husband?"

"I want to dance all night, then take you on the floor next to a crackling fireplace."

She smirked—not that he could see. "Is that a line?"

"The fuck if I know—it's just what I want."

She sat on the couch next to him. He wasted no time in pulling her into his arms.

"Hike your skirt up." Before she could reply, his fingers were already doing the work.

"Bennings will be in here at any moment."

"Yes, and then we'll be in the car for an hour until we get to the airport. And then we'll be on a plane for three or four hours. And then Scotty will have to be fed and put to bed." She knew he was exasperated. "Do you get what I'm saying, wifey? I've only had you for a week now, and I don't know that we've made a baby of our own yet."

Hazel wasn't too sure of that. They'd never used protection all the times they had made love—even before the marriage. For the past few days, she'd woken up overly nauseous. But she didn't want to say anything yet or even see a doctor yet. Not while they were in the manor. Not while they were in St. Jerome.

She'd find out in New York. In her heart, though, she was pretty sure she knew the answer.

"Ahem, Mr. John, the town car is here for us." Hazel hopped out of John's arms and smoothed down her skirt.

"Did you call your mother and tell her the news?"

"Not yet. I'll tell her when we're in New York." Though Hazel knew that would be an uncomfortable conversation.

Or not.

After all, she hadn't repeated her mother's mistakes this time around. She had reclaimed what was almost lost to her. Now Scotty had a father, and she would give John another child.

"I can't wait to meet your mother."

She cracked a laugh. "Oh, you say that now, but just you wait."

The memories of her life as Alison were getting clearer, but she still relied on John heavily to fill in some of the blanks. Bennings's drinking problem, for one. It bothered her a lot that she could barely recall Alison's childhood. But from what John had said, it was a messy business of living with an alcoholic father and then moving to a foster home. Maybe it was a blessing she couldn't remember that part. It wasn't as though she could remember those first few years as Hazel Loveless either.

It was the new memories that she wanted to focus on. The past represented too much pain for both of them. The present was what they would build on. If everything went smoothly in New York, their future would be solid. No more darkness. No more black water.

Hazel and John both still clung to one piece of the past—the fateful silver charm. For a wedding present, Hazel had taken the charm to a jeweler. The charm was split in half and welded into two perfectly smoothed medallions. Both she and John wore them around their necks, not as anchors to the past but as tethers to each other.

After an hour, the town car was packed. Bennings sat in the front seat with the driver. John, Hazel, and Scotty sat in the back.

As the view of the manor grew dimmer behind them, Hazel breathed a sigh of relief. Then she remembered the check. She had shoved it in her coat pocket. Carefully, she unwadded it and placed it in John's hand.

"Your check, I'm giving it back to you."

"Why? It's your money anyway."

"I know, but technically I didn't stay the full month."

He scoffed. "Multiple crises, hospital trips, and wedding shopping don't count."

"You made the terms, my love." She paused as the car sped over the newly repaired bridge. It felt as if the veil had finally been lifted from her eyes. The sun was suddenly shining brighter.

She watched John. He seemed almost stricken for a moment. He pulled his sunglasses off and squinted his eyes toward the sun.

"John? Are you alright?"

+++

He stopped squinting and started smiling. Then he turned and looked at her—*looked* at her!

"John? You're frightening me."

He patted her on the cheek, then glanced down and kissed the top of Scotty's head. Their daughter beamed a smile back up at him.

"John, what—"

"I can see you, Hazel Stonem. I can see you. I can see Scotty." He reached over Scotty and kissed Hazel passionately. "I can see you, wifey. I can see you!"

As the manor faded farther and farther behind them, John's sight returned in full. There was no limit to the emotions that flooded through him. He had everything. He had his wife. He had a new daughter. And life, after all those years in hell, was suddenly sunshiny again.

Maybe an evil spell had been cast on John and Alison Stonem. Maybe the debt to break the spell was John's twenty years of grief and Hazel's resilience against any and all obstacles. Eternal love: what a simple solution.

Neither Hazel nor John bothered to speculate too hard. Life was too good to dwell on the past. Late August in New York brought a new daughter to the cozy Stonem home.

John was overwhelmed by what he felt for the tiny newborn. Barely a month after his adoption of Scotty was finalized, he now had two daughters. As he opened the door to their apartment, he was careful to let Hazel inside first. Scotty was sitting on the sofa looking anxious to hold her new sister.

"Hope Stonem," Hazel crooned, "welcome home."

"Perfectly named," Bennings chimed in.

"I couldn't agree more." John was gushing with love. It was love they were all living on.

Their home wasn't an extravagant or even a large apartment— but it was perfect for two little girls, their devoted parents, and a former butler who was permanently promoted to grandfather.

There could be a happy ending after all.

Epilogue

Subject: Stonem Manor
From: margaret.thornberry@aol.com
To: jmstonem@stonemindustries.com
Dear Mr. John and Mrs. Hazel,

It alarms me to report that your lovely house continues to fall into disrepair. I'm continually hiring new people—some of them, I apologize, not as professional as they ought to be. But as I say, Mr. John, people don't seem to want to have anything to do with this place now.

There are lots of reports of screaming and nasty laughter—mostly from the fourth floor. I did as you instructed and closed off the rooms on that floor, but the laughter and screams continue to taunt me and the rest of the staff.

Last week, Mrs. Bruce (our newest cook) found a rather strange-looking doll lying in the middle of the hallway up there. She retrieved it, thinking it should be donated to the children's charity, and placed it in the donation box, which was clearly labeled with the pink and blue adhesive tape that you yourself use, sir. The tops of the boxes were then secured with packing tape. Later in the day, Mrs. Bruce thought she heard laughter coming from the fourth floor. When she went up to investigate, she found the doll—yes, the very same doll—sitting against the wall at the end of the hall.

Mrs. Bruce has not returned since telling me of this.

I write to you in earnest, sir, to request that you either return and see that we haven't all gone bonkers, or that the house be abandoned and the lot of us allowed to leave. My request may seem extreme, but the increasing strangeness has us all quite afraid. We do understand if our employment with the Stonem family cannot be saved.

Respectfully,
Margaret Thornberry
Subject: RE: Stonem Manor

From: jmstonem@stonemindustries.com
To: margaret.thornberry@aol.com

Margaret,

*Gather up the others and get the hell out of there—immediately.
That's an order. I'll be in touch shortly with reassignments.*

Regards,
J. Stonem
P.S. Leave the doll.

ABOUT THE AUTHOR

Lana Moon grew up in Southeast Missouri. She has a background in medieval and American folklore, and spent a brief period moonlighting as a ghost hunter. When that group dissolved, she still had a strong desire to explore old buildings and abandoned properties in Missouri and Illinois. As a result, many of these "forgotten" places are settings in her stories.

Moon has been writing for more than a decade and she contributes regularly to the Shorties blog (darkanddirtyorigins.blogspot.com), which features free short stories and book excerpts.

Did you enjoy this book? Drop us a line and say so! We love to hear from readers, and so do our authors. To connect, visit www.boroughspublishinggroup.com online, send comments directly to info@boroughspublishinggroup.com, or friend us on Facebook and Twitter. And be sure to check back regularly for contests and new releases in your favorite subgenres of romance!

Are you an aspiring writer? Check out www.boroughspublishinggroup.com/submit and see if we can help you make your dreams come true.

www.ingramcontent.com/pod-product-compliance
Lightning Source LLC
Chambersburg PA
CBHW070843120626
46556CB00002B/854